*Wednesday, October 12th*

'Is the whole world going mad?

I was driving to work this morning on my scooter when the driver of a Ford Cortina wound his window down and spat a piece of apple core straight into my lap.

"Excuse me," I called out as we drew level at the traffic lights, "that went on me." He looked at me for a moment, threw the rest of his half-eaten apple at me, and drove off up the Bayswater Road. I was so busy trying to remember his number that I drove into the back of the car in front. . . . As if I didn't have enough to worry about.'

D0522823

# Diary of a Somebody

## CHRISTOPHER MATTHEW

### Illustrated by Peter Brookes

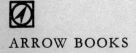

ARROW BOOKS

For Robert Morley

Arrow Books Limited
3 Fitzroy Square, London W 1 P 6 J D

An imprint of the Hutchinson Publishing Group

London Melbourne Sydney Auckland
Wellington Johannesburg and agencies
throughout the world

First published by Hutchinson 1978
Arrow edition 1980
Reprinted 1980
Reprinted 1981

Text © Christopher Matthew 1978
Illustrations © Hutchinson Publishing Group Ltd 1978

The author acknowledges assistance from the
Arts Council of Great Britain.

This book is sold subject to the condition that it
shall not, by way of trade or otherwise, be lent,
resold, hired out, or otherwise circulated without
the publisher's prior consent in any form of
binding or cover other than that in which it is
published and without a similar condition including this condition being imposed on the
subsequent purchaser

Made and printed in Great Britain
by The Anchor Press Ltd
Tiptree, Essex

ISBN 0 09 921500 4

# September

## Friday, September 2nd

I have decided it is high time I started to keep a diary. I simply cannot imagine why I have not done so before. When I think of the many interesting things that have happened to me over the years, I can only curse myself for not having had the sense to jot them all down.

I have travelled a fair amount – in Europe mainly – and come into contact with many interesting people, some of whom have been quite famous in their way. I cannot pretend that Simon Crisp is a household name, but that is not to say that the people I meet and the places I go to are any the less interesting for that. Indeed, in my opinion, fame can very often be a disadvantage in a diarist.

I do not suppose for a moment that anyone would wish to go so far as to publish my observations on life, and anyone who thinks that is why I have decided to start a diary could not be further off the mark. On the other hand, it might be interesting for my grandchildren and their children to browse through in years to come, and get some idea of how life in England was lived in the late 1970s. If ever I get married, that is.

Everyone in the flat is of the opinion that thirty-five is too old to be thinking of starting a diary. I cannot agree with them there and have made my opinions felt in no uncertain terms. I have never subscribed to this widely held theory that you have to have reached a certain stage in your career by a certain age in order to be considered a success. Look at Margaret Rutherford. She did not set foot on a stage until she was over thirty. And Milton waited till he was an old man before starting work on *Paradise Lost.*

## Saturday, September 3rd

To Smith's to buy a diary. One of those substantial ones with a lock, I thought. Astonished to discover that the only diaries they had in stock were for next year. When I asked the woman at the desk for one for this year, she laughed and replied that they had sold out months ago. I said that, as far as I was concerned, we were still very much in this year, and that there must be many people who decide to start diaries in September. She said she had never heard of anyone doing it. I replied that it was extremely narrow-minded to assume that the year begins for everyone on January 1st and ends on December 31st.

'Narrow-minded it may be,' she retorted, 'but for everyone I know it does.'

'Even the Persians?' I asked.

She said that she was happy to say that she did not know any Persians, and what was more, I was holding up the queue. I pointed out that London had a large Persian population these days, and the sooner people like her came to terms with the fact, the better would be our chances of cheaper petrol.

'Well, all I can say is,' she snapped, 'they obviously don't keep diaries.'

'That makes two of you,' I said, and left.

No wonder big business in this country is in the doldrums if that is the way large firms carry on. And to think that only thirty-eight years ago to this day, we went to war with Germany. There is obviously nothing for it but to use a notebook, at least for the time being, but it is really far from satisfactory.

Arrived back in the flat just as Jane was leaving in true secretarial style to spend the weekend at her parents' in Oxted. If only she would do something about her hair. I am not surprised she has such difficulty finding a boyfriend. Her skin leaves much to be desired, too.

After tea, a couple of Victoria's weird friends came to take her off to one of their Workers' Workshops, whatever they may be. I fail to understand what an attractive, well-educated girl like her, with wealthy parents in Berkshire and a decent job in an art gallery, can possibly see in all this namby-pamby, lefty nonsense. I have tried to talk her out of it on several occasions, but I might just as well save my breath. If I didn't want to run the risk of looking like a fortune hunter, I might seriously consider setting my cap at her. She is very much my type.

Beddoes had his latest girlfriend Jackie round in the evening, and monopolized the television set again, to say nothing of the settee. If he must devote his spare time to a temporary waitress from Shepherd's Bush, at least he might get her to help out a bit at meal times. I do not mind cooking pork chops and vegetables for three people, but I do draw the line at being treated like a skivvy.

I restrained my feelings until the time came to bring the coffee in, when I banged Jackie's down on the table – rather too hard, as it turned out, since the cup tipped over, spilling coffee all down my trousers. I immediately sponged them with cold water and can only hope for the best.

## Sunday, September 4th

Woken at nine by Beddoes knocking loudly on my door and calling out that he and Jackie were just off for the day to Brighton and there was no milk in the fridge. What he omitted to mention was that they had also finished off the rest of the loaf and covered most of the sink and draining board with a thin coating of burnt toast scrapings. How a man like that manages to hold down a responsible job in the City when he is incapable of calculating the number of slices in a loaf of bread is beyond me.

Victoria's political soirée had apparently turned into an all-night affair. Why I should feel so jealous of a bunch of second-rate Commies I simply cannot imagine, but I do.

I am definitely beginning to regret now that I asked her out to dinner on Monday night.

The coffee stain has still not come out of my trousers.

## Monday, September 5th

A curious thing happened today in the office. Shortly after lunch, Armitage stuck his head round the door of the outer office just as I was dictating an important letter to Sarah, our new secretary, and said, 'Oh, by the way, if reception calls up to say Audrey Hepburn is here, ask them to send her straight up, will you?'

Not surprisingly, everyone was very excited at the news that the famous star was expected at any minute, and one or two began tidying their desks. Iversen even went so far as to slip out and have his hair cut.

I said to Sarah that I never realized Armitage knew Audrey Hepburn, to which she replied, 'Why shouldn't he? As the chairman's nephew I expect he gets to meet all sorts of interesting and important people down on his uncle's yacht on the Hamble.'

No matter how badly Armitage behaves, it is impossible to fault him in Sarah's eyes. She seems besotted by him, though heaven knows why.

More out of idle curiosity than from any genuine desire to meet the actress, I put off a couple of not very important meetings. I also rang Victoria to say that I might be a little late for our dinner date.

By five-thirty there was still no sign of Miss Hepburn, and at six, Armitage stuck his head round the door and said, 'Oh well, it doesn't look as though she'll be coming now, does it? Anyway, I'm off now. Good night, laddie.'

Arrived home to find a note from Victoria saying that she couldn't be fished to wait around any longer and had gone to the pictures with Beddoes. So much for left-wing manners.

## Tuesday, September 6th

Have been thinking about this Audrey Hepburn business all day and can only assume it was meant to be one of Armitage's so-called jokes. If so, it certainly didn't cut much ice with me. On the other hand, I suppose there is no reason why he shouldn't have been telling the truth. The problem now is to find out if he was, without giving the impression that I give two hoots one way or another.

On the way in to work, I took the opportunity of button-holing George, the commissionaire, and asking him if by chance he had happened to see Audrey Hepburn going in or out of the building yesterday.

He thought for a while, then said, 'Audrey Hepburn, sir? Would she be with the frozen-food people?'

Either he knows something I don't, or else he has never been near a cinema in his life. Either way, it's decidedly rum. Asked Victoria out to dinner tomorrow night and she has accepted.

## Wednesday, September 7th

Looking forward to taking Victoria out to dinner so much that I was scarcely able to bend my mind to anything else all day. When Sarah came back from the coffee machine this morning, I found to my amazement that I had asked for hot chocolate, a drink I have not touched since childhood and heartily detest.

Decided to book up at a restaurant near Balham called The Soup Kitchen. Tim and Vanessa Pedalow recommended it and said that the last time they had been there, Prince Charles had been a fellow diner. They hadn't actually seen him themselves, but they had been told by one of the waiters that he was there somewhere. The theme of the restaurant, I gathered, was the American Depression – everything very plain and basic, especially the food. It definitely sounded the sort of thing that would suit Victoria with her proletarian views.

Unfortunately, we took rather longer to find it than I had anticipated, as a result of which they had given away our table, thinking we weren't coming, and we had to take a bowl each and stand in a queue outside in the street until a table became free. Luckily it wasn't too cold, although I was thankful I had brought a light overcoat. Victoria said it took the chill off her shoulders very nicely. After about ten minutes, she was all for leaving and finding somewhere else. However, I assured her that it was really well worth the wait, and at that moment a waiter in faded black trousers and a stained white shirt came out and told us he had a table for two ready. I was sorry we were not able to sit in the main part of the restaurant and spot the famous writers and TV actors who, according to Tim and Vanessa, use the place as their canteen. On the other hand, it was quite cosy and intimate behind the pillar, even if it was a little difficult to catch the waiter's eye.

When I did finally manage to hail one and ask him for a menu, he told me, rather rudely I thought, that it was chalked up on the wall on the far side of the room. I went to have a look, and when I came back, told Victoria that I would be going for the vegetable soup followed by the cheese omelette. She replied that, in that case, she would certainly choose the most expensive and exotic thing on the menu. I pointed out that that *was* the most exotic and expensive thing on the menu and that the whole point of the place was that everything was very much in keeping with the hard times we were living through.

She looked round at the rather stark grey walls and the plain wooden tables and said, 'What's this place called again?'

I told her The Soup Kitchen.

She said, 'The Soup Outside Loo would be a better name for it. Even the seats are round, hard and cold.'

I said that I thought *she* was being a bit hard, but she didn't seem to get the joke.

The soup, when it finally came, was quite tasty if a little tepid, and there were very nearly words when the waiter – accidentally, Victoria said; I still claim on purpose – shot an entire cheese omelette straight into my lap.

Victoria remarked, 'This sort of thing never happens at the Savoy Grill.'

I asked her when was the last time she had dined at the Savoy Grill, and she said that she and the others often popped in there for a bite after one of their Workers' Workshop meetings. I was astounded and said that that was hardly the behaviour one expected from socialists.

'We believe in spreading the money around instead of wasting our time salving our consciences by occasional bouts of pseudo-poverty,' she said.

I was dumbstruck, though not half so much as I was by the bill when it finally arrived. For that price we might just as well have gone to the Savoy Grill. At least we would not have gone home still feeling hungry, and I might now be on speaking terms with Victoria.

I only hope the egg stains come out better than the coffee.

## Thursday, September 8th

Astonished to receive a telephone call from Mike Pritchard, of all people, asking if he could pop round and see me after supper on a matter of some delicacy. I doubt if I have exchanged a dozen words with him since we were at Oxford together nearly fifteen years ago. He had always seemed slightly older than the rest of us in the JCR, but nothing had prepared me for the balding, middle-aged figure to whom I opened the door this evening.

'Wizard,' he said as I showed him into the sitting room. Victoria and Jane were there with plates of scrambled eggs perched on their knees.

I introduced them to Mike who said, 'Wizard. I wouldn't mind seeing the news if that's all right by you.'

And before I could say a word, he marched forward and plumped himself down into the best armchair. I asked him if he would like some coffee, whereupon he produced two bottles of claret from inside his anorak and banged them down on the table saying, 'This'll do you more good than coffee any day.' Picking up a nearby glass he then proceeded to pour himself a large measure. 'Wizard,' he said, leaning back with his nose over the rim of the glass. 'Well, what have you been up to since we last met?' Before I could utter a word, he launched into a long account of his own recent life.

It appeared that his marriage had not been a success. He is now divorced from Babs and living in digs in Clapham. He has two children, Tom aged eight and Gerry (short for Geraldine) aged twelve, who stay with him at weekends. I'm not surprised he arrives at work on Monday mornings absolutely exhausted. He has already lost two good jobs in industry and looks set fair to lose a third. Even so, I was rather taken aback when he suggested I might be kind enough to look after the children for the day on Saturday, and the pretext of a slight acquaintance at university seemed decidedly thin. However, it is the least I can do. Besides, who knows, it might be rather an interesting experience to have to look after two children for a day. A sort of simulated parenthood.

Mike was obviously relieved when I agreed. 'Wizard,' he said, and drained the bottle. Then he got up to go.

Assuming he had left the second bottle as a sort of thank-you present, but not wishing to take it for granted, I said,

'Oh, you seem to have left something behind.' 'Oh, so I have,' he said, picked up the bottle and left the room.

In the hall he bumped into Victoria who was on the way to the bathroom in her nightie, and immediately invited her to have dinner with him in a 'cheap and cheerful little place' he had discovered in Kennington, specializing in different types of stew. To my astonishment, she agreed. I give up.

## Friday, September 9th

Was on my way out to lunch when the lift stopped at the fourth floor, and in stepped Armitage, laughing rather too loudly, as usual, and a couple of his rugger-playing cronies – Prout from Accounts and Attenborough from Merchandising Development.

He nodded at me in a superior way and said, 'Basement for you, I presume?' at which the other two sniggered.

I decided it was high time he was taken down a peg or two, so I remarked casually, 'Funny about Audrey Hepburn not turning up the other evening, wasn't it?'

Prout said, 'What's all this then, Col?'

They both looked at him expectantly.

'Oh,' said Armitage, 'did I say Audrey Hepburn? How silly of me. I meant, of course, Katherine Hepburn.'

The others seemed rather baffled, as well they might be. It's hopeless trying to carry on a sensible conversation with Armitage when he's in that sort of mood, and so I maintained a dignified silence.

As we were leaving the building, there was some horseplay with the swing doors as a result of which I missed a perfectly good taxi and had to travel to my lunch date by underground.

## Saturday, September 10th

Woke early with a shock to realize that I had accepted an invitation to Nick and Warthog's wedding in Newbury. Rang Mike at eight but there was no reply. Had barely replaced the receiver when there was a ring at the front door and there he was with the children, both dressed in jeans and T-shirts. Tom's had a finger on his, pointing towards his sister, with the words: THIS IDIOT'S WITH ME. Surprised to see she was much more grown up for her age than I had imagined.

I explained my problem re the wedding, but all Mike said was, 'Wizard, they enjoy weddings.'

And without another word he strode off down the corridor. Arrived at the church rather later than I had hoped. As we were being shown to our seats, I noticed a number of guests whispering and giggling. I looked down and realized that the finger on Tom's T-shirt was pointing at me. I gave them all a cold stare and took my place. As I was leaning forward to pray, I overbalanced slightly on the narrow seat, banging my forehead against the back of the woman's head in the pew in front and knocking her hat slightly askew.

In the middle of the service, just as the couple were making their marriage vows, I suddenly realized that, by an astonishing coincidence, the vicar had been at the same college as me at Oxford. Afterwards I went up to him and made myself known, but he did not remember me at all. However, now I come to think about it, although we were certainly contemporaries, I don't believe we ever actually spoke. At the reception I overheard a stout woman in a mauve hat confiding to a small, dried-up-looking man that Nick had only married Warthog – or Margaret, as she called her – for her money. This was the first I had heard of Warthog's family having the sort of money people marry for. Even if it were true, it does not seem to me to be a sound basis on which to build a happy and lasting union. But that is only my opinion.

The children behaved extremely well, helping to carry round trays of eats and refilling people's glasses. It was a pity Tom had to go and blot his copybook, not to say Warthog's mother's white shoes, by making himself sick on Coca-Cola, but people could not have been more understanding – especially Warthog's mother who assured me that her little woman in the village was a positive genius with stains.

As we were leaving, I caught my foot on the top of the front-door steps and stumbled forward, giving another departing guest a sharp blow on the back of his head with my elbow, and knocking his top hat to the ground. When he turned round, I saw that it was the husband of the woman whose hat I had dislodged in the church. I did not see that there was any call to be quite so offensive. It was only an accident.

Tom was sick again in the car going home. Thank heaven for Volkswagen's rubber floors.

## Sunday, September 11th

A potentially good night's sleep disturbed by the most extraordinarily erotic dreams about Geraldine. I have been able to think of nothing else all day.

Beddoes, as usual, stayed in bed with Jackie all day,

'As we were leaving I caught my foot on the top of the front doorsteps and stumbled forward . . .'

emerging finally in time for a drink at six-thirty. Is it any wonder one has erotic dreams when this is the sort of atmosphere one has to live in? The sooner I discourage Pritchard from landing me with his children again, the better for all our sakes. Apart from anything else, I see no reason why I should be made a convenience of.

## Monday, September 12th

Quite unable to sleep all night for thinking about Geraldine. As a result, arrived at the office exhausted.

'You look as though you had a skinful over the weekend,' Armitage called out as I passed his office, and laughed coarsely – as too did Sarah. She seems to be in there with him all the time nowadays. I am seriously thinking of saying something about it. While reading through the Barford projected sales figures before lunch, I fell fast asleep and would probably have slept until five-thirty had my elbow not slipped off the edge of the desk, bringing my chin down with a sharp crack on my blotter.

After lunch Uncle Ted rang to say he was in town for the day to see his accountant, and would I care to join him at the Athenaeum for tea?

Went straight in to see Roundtree, our group head, with some excuse about having a dentist appointment, and left at once for the Athenaeum.

An unpleasant scene with the porter at the side entrance who claimed to have no knowledge whatever of a Mr Rathbone. I made no secret of my irritation and pointed out sharply that he had been a member for forty years. 'Not of this club, sir,' said the porter impassively.

I finally had to tell him that I had expected something better of the Athenaeum. 'This is the Travellers,' he said. 'The Athenaeum is next door.' The situation was not made any easier by the fact that the chap was coloured.

After tea I set off home on my scooter, only to find the Mall solid with traffic, all heading towards Admiralty Arch. It was not until I reached Parliament Square that I discovered the reason the whole of central London had been brought to a virtual standstill was a demonstration by large numbers of ugly and ill-dressed men and women swarming all over the road carrying banners with such slogans as FIGHT THE

CUTS, SAVE JOBS and CUTS BASH GAYS. I have no idea what they were all on about, and I'd be the last person to condemn minority groups, but I wouldn't have minded bashing a few gays myself at that moment, and one or two others while I was about it.

Fortunately, thanks to some deft manoeuvring on my scooter, I was able to get in in time for the 'Six O'Clock News'. Even so, as I said to Jane in the kitchen that evening, the day decent, law-abiding citizens are no longer able to get home to their wives and loved ones after a hard day's work, it'll be the end of civilized life in this country as we know it.

As I might have expected, she took me far too literally and said, 'But you haven't got a wife or any loved ones,' which I thought was rather unkind. At that moment, Victoria walked in, and before long, heated words were being exchanged. 'I give up,' she said finally. 'It is quite obvious to me that you are, politically speaking, totally naive – and probably sexually impotent.' And she marched out, slamming the door behind her with such force that she cracked one of the frosted glass panels. I suppose I'll have to pay for that, as usual.

Later, to my surprise, she came to my room as I was lying in bed reading and said if I thought she had come to apologize, I'd another think coming, but that if I'd be interested in accompanying her to the following night's Workers' Workshop Session, I'd be very welcome. I said I'd think about it.

## Tuesday, September 13th

Another restless night, thanks to a recurring dream that I was having tea with Lenin in the hallway of the Travellers Club. Awoke exhausted but enthusiastic about Victoria's invitation. I think perhaps I *am* a little out of touch with left-wing thought in this country and a glimpse, however brief, into how the other half thinks, could be only an advantage. On the way into work, bought a copy of the *Morning Star*, but left it behind on the tube before I'd had a chance to read a word of it.

For some reason had always imagined that Workers' Workshop meetings were held in a dingy basement room in the Gray's Inn Road. Was most surprised, therefore, to find myself in the sitting room of an expensively decorated flat in Covent Garden belonging to a smooth-faced man with carefully brushed grey hair and a double-breasted dove-grey suit by the name of Terry. I did not catch his other name, but he looked a bit of a nancy boy to me. At all events, he is certainly not my idea of a typical member of the English working classes.

In fact I doubt if any of them would have recognized a worker if he had walked in through the window. Nevertheless, they all talked at great length about the Englishman's right to work, and the dignity of human labour. I felt tempted to express the alternative view on several occasions, but since I was a guest, it seemed rude to interrupt. At eleven biscuits and hot chocolate were served, and a protest deploring the government's failure to reduce the level of unemployment was handed round for everyone to sign. I have never been very keen on the idea of putting my name to documents of any kind. However, not wishing to cause any ructions back in the flat, I decided not to make an issue of it. I had considered signing a false name, but in the end I wrote down my own, but very indistinctly.

As we were leaving, Terry took my hand and gave it a little squeeze. 'Britain needs people like you,' he said softly, 'and so do I.'

I'm pretty certain he's a pansy.

Was going to say something about it to Victoria on the way home, when suddenly she exclaimed, 'There's a horrible smell in this car. If you don't mind, I'll get out here and catch a taxi.'

I suppose I had better give the floor another going over. As if I didn't have enough on my hands.

## Wednesday, September 14th

Woke in the middle of the night in a cold sweat about this thing I signed last night. What if it should ever fall into the hands of the Special Branch? Or worse still, supposing this country were ever to be taken over by a right-wing dictatorship, which is quite possible in my view? How am I ever going to explain to the Secret Police that I only signed it for domestic reasons? I know I signed my name illegibly, but was it illegible enough? Just to be on the safe side, every time the phone rang today in my office, I answered in a disguised voice. Once I gave such a good imitation of a

West Indian that I had Roundtree fooled for several minutes.

Later, Betty from Accounts rang, so I tried it out again on her, and launched into a long, satirical account of last night's events in Covent Garden. Suddenly I was interrupted by this woman's voice shrieking, 'You double-crossing, superior Fascist bastard. I'll get even with you for this.'

It's funny, but I had never realized before how similar Betty and Victoria sound on the phone.

I knew I should have left politics well alone.

## Thursday, September 15th

I do not earn a particularly high salary, but I'd give ten pounds to know who sewed up the bottom of my pyjama trousers. I think I have a pretty fair idea, but no firm evidence. It's not the torn ends I mind so much as the sprained toe I received when I first drove my foot unwittingly into the leg.

## Saturday, September 17th

To the National to see the Robert Bolt play about the Russian Revolution. Rather an apt choice in the circumstances. In the interval ran into the Pedalows who were at the Olivier seeing *The Plough and the Stars*. Vanessa said, 'Oh, we saw the Bolt when it first opened. I thought it rather a superficial view of what was, after all, the turning point of modern civilization.'

I didn't like to say so, but I thought it was very deep and at times quite difficult to follow – though not half as difficult as filling out the advance booking form, which is like sitting an entrance test for MENSA. I would have mentioned the matter to Peter Hall on the way out had he not been in conversation. 'We've had problems,' I heard him saying, 'like you wouldn't believe.' The fact that we have as the head of our National Theatre a man who cannot speak grammatical English I find far from reassuring.

## Sunday, September 18th

An overcast day. In an effort to get rid of the nasty smell in the car, I tried a particularly strong type of cleaner, and after swabbing it all over the offending area, left it for a couple of hours to soak. When I came back, I found that it had dissolved the rubber and started eating into the metal floor underneath, leaving behind an even more unpleasant smell than before.

My toe is, if anything, worse.

## Monday, September 19th

At lunchtime decided to try a new bistro that has just opened in the next street to the office. It is one of those places on several floors. Thought I'd try the basement. On the way down, who should I see sitting alone at a table for four but Hugh Bryant-Fenn.

When I asked him what he was up to, he said, 'Oh, I'm doing the restaurant column in *Bedroom*.'

It was all gobbledygook to me until he explained that *Bedroom* was a new magazine starting up, similar to *Penthouse* and *Mayfair*. 'The articles are frightful,' he said cheerfully, 'but the girls are fantastic.'

This was surprising news, since the last time I had met him at the Pedalows he had just set up as an interior design consultant with an office in Beauchamp Place. 'I see,' I said, 'so *that's* why you're here?'

'Why?' he said.

'To write this place up for your *Bedroom* column?'

'Good Lord, no,' he said. 'I wouldn't put this place in my column if they paid me. Which they do, as a matter of fact.'

He went on to explain in a confidential way that he was about to meet a chap to talk about the possibility of presenting Diana Ross and the Supremes for a season in the Rose Room at Bourne and Hollingsworth. I said that I had understood that Diana Ross had split up with the Supremes some years ago.

Bryant-Fenn tapped the side of his nose and leaned forward confidentially. 'Wait and see, chum,' he murmured, 'wait and see.'

Bryant-Fenn was still there as I was leaving – only now he was deep in conversation with two rather tarty-looking blonde girls wearing too much make-up. Whatever their professions, they didn't look to me the sort of people who'd know anything about presenting Diana Ross and the Supremes in the Rose Room of Bourne and Hollingsworth, or anywhere else. Not wishing to put Hugh on a spot, I tried to slip by without his noticing. However, he called me over and taking a card out of his pocket said, 'You look the sort of person who could make use of this. Take a few friends. If there's any trouble just mention my name.'

When I got outside I saw it was a printed invitation to a free meal at a restaurant called the Botticelli – somewhere in St John's Wood. I doubt if I shall ever be able to take advantage of it; but still, it was decent of him to think I might. In the bus going home this evening, some woman dropped an extremely heavy bag of shopping right on my bad toe. She looked Arabic, I thought.

## Tuesday, September 20th

Was on the point of tackling a boiled egg at breakfast this morning when I happened to notice that the Picasso poster which hangs above the table had slipped down between the glass and the hardboard backing. I stood up, leaned forward across the table, and took hold of the glass frame which immediately split right down the middle. Not only does this mean I shall now have to have a new piece of glass cut, but since there was a very real possibility that glass splinters had fallen into my boiled egg, I had to throw it away along with the butter that was on my plate. Unfortunately, since I was by then rather late for work, there was no time to boil another egg. In addition, I discovered that we were out of butter. I only hope that broken picture glass does not carry the same curse as a broken mirror.

My toe is no better.

## Wednesday, September 21st

I have been thinking: this free meal invitation of Bryant-Fenn's is obviously just a PR gimmick to drum up trade for the restaurant. It surely cannot matter to them *who* takes up the offer as long as *someone* does.

After lunch, rang the Pedalows who have had me to dinner several times lately to ask them to join me. 'How divine,' said Vanessa in her squeaky voice. 'You'd better check with monsieur first, though. I'll put you through to the study.'

'Sounds all right,' said Tim in his usual off-hand way.

'Just check the old almanac . . . No problem. I'm not going to Australia now till next week.'

Those two are a complete mystery to me. They have obviously made a lot of money but no one seems to know how. Hugh says he thinks it's something to do with land speculation. I thought he was meant to be a stockbroker. I have also invited Roundtree's secretary, Felicity. I wouldn't at all mind starting something up with her. She has a magnificent figure, and her accent is not really as bad as all that. Would have asked Victoria, but as she has refused point-blank to speak to me for a week, it's rather difficult.

## Thursday, September 22nd

Our evening at the Botticelli started off very well. Tim and Vanessa seemed very much at home there, and spent a lot of time waving to people they knew. They seemed slightly surprised that the waiters kept calling me Mr Bryant-Fenn, but I explained that it was Hugh who had recommended the place to me and booked our table. Felicity obviously went down extremely well, at least with Tim who could hardly tear his eyes away from her bust. It was a pity that, as she has clearly never read a book or been to a play in her life, she was able to contribute very little to the conversation. However, she showed interest, which is the main thing.

The restaurant itself was decorated in a typically self-conscious style, I thought. Dark brown walls, potted plants everywhere, limited editions in silver frames and a great deal of indirect lighting. Remarked on this to Vanessa who said, 'Oh, we like it.' They would.

Wondered if they would have been as keen on the prices, which were steep, to say the least. Fortunately, however, cost was not on this occasion my concern, and we all did ourselves extremely proud: smoked salmon to start with, followed by veally things and salad. We had three bottles of Hospices de Beaune 1969 and brandy and liqueurs afterwards. I also decided, just for once, to join Tim in a large Romeo y Julietta. When the waiter brought the bill, I discreetly slipped him the invitation card and returned at once to the conversation. The waiter, however, instead of bustling about his business, tapped me on the shoulder and, holding up the card, asked in a loud voice what this was meant to be. I explained in a low voice that it was all perfectly in order. However, he insisted that he knew nothing about it, so I suggested he address any queries to the manager. I assumed that was the end of that, but a minute or two later he was back again, this time with the manager – a superior-looking fellow who was all olive skin and sideboards.

'Excuse me, sir,' he said, 'but was this given to you by TCP Public Relations?' I took a bow at a venture, and replied that it was. 'Oh, I'm very sorry, sir,' said the manager, 'but TCP stopped handling our account over three months ago. Under the circumstances, Mr Fern, I could possibly see my way to giving you a slight discount – say five per cent . . . ?'

I was on the point of suggesting we might discuss the matter elsewhere, when Tim said, 'That'll be all right, Gino. Just put it on my account.'

Gino said, 'Yes, of course, Mr Pedalow. Good evening, Mrs Pedalow. It's always a pleasure to welcome *old friends* to the Botticelli.'

I doubt if I have felt more humiliated in my life. I made it quite clear to Tim that I considered his offer to be merely a loan and told him I should be sending a cheque in the morning.

Felicity did not say much during all this, but I shall be astonished if the news is not all round the office by lunchtime tomorrow.

## Friday, September 23rd

The instant I got in this morning, I was on the phone to Bryant-Fenn to say that he owed me an apology and £88·00. To my astonishment he feigned ignorance and innocence; and to add insult to injury, when I told him that his invitation was totally worthless, all he could find to say was, 'Oh. So you had to stump up then?'

I explained that Tim had very kindly come to my rescue, thus saving us all further embarrassment.

'It would seem to me,' Hugh said, 'that if I owe anyone eighty-eight pounds it's Tim.'

I said that was not the point.

'I don't understand,' he said, interrupting me rudely. 'You got a free meal out of it, didn't you? I don't see you have anything to complain about.'

I put the phone down on him. I have always said that public relations attracted the second-rate, and am only glad that I have nothing to do with it.

Returned from lunch to find a note pinned to my office door saying: 'How to Eat Out at the Best Restaurants Free in One Easy Lesson. Apply: S. Crisp. Ext. 7440 (Reversed charge calls not accepted).' The message was unsigned, but I detect the hand of Armitage in this. I shall certainly not give him the satisfaction of thinking I even noticed it.

## Saturday, September 24th

Yet another reference in the paper to this chap who's leaving the Labour Party. If my experiences in Covent Garden last week are anything to go by, I can't say I'm entirely surprised. I wonder that intelligent men should ever join in the first place.

Jackie came round again this evening and made an enormous spaghetti for herself and Beddoes. I do not mind her not making enough for me, and am perfectly prepared to believe she thought I was out, but how she manages to get short lengths of uncooked spaghetti all over the kitchen floor is beyond me. I went in there after they had gone to bed to cook myself a boiled egg, skidded on the spaghetti which rolled under my feet and came down with a crash, catching the back of my head against the door frame.

Jane, who arrived on the scene at that moment, could not have been more helpful, dabbing Dettol on the bump and making me a cup of tea. We talked for quite a long time together afterwards in the sitting room. Although obviously very shy with men, she has a good sense of humour. All it needs is for someone to bring it out. The sad fact is, though, that she will never get anywhere until she does something about her complexion.

Noticed in the bath tonight that my toenail is beginning to turn quite black.

## Monday, September 26th

At dinner at the Varney-Birches', I was introduced to a girl who said, 'Are you by any chance related to the Smith's Crisps?'

I presume she was trying to be funny, but you can never really tell with those sort of people.

## Tuesday, September 27th

To Leeds on the train with Armitage and Roundtree to look round the Barford set-up. Their marketing chap, Neville Pratt, travelled with us. A more tedious and fruitless exercise it would be hard to imagine.

On the way back to the station to catch the evening train, we called in the bar of the Metropole for a quick drink. Who should be there but Bryant-Fenn who announced that he had been up in Leeds to give a talk to a local literary society on Dante Gabriel Rossetti.

When I expressed surprise, he said, 'Oh, I do quite a bit of lecturing, you know, up and down the country. Mainly to ladies' luncheon clubs. It's quite a good racket. Sixty quid in cash and a first-class return rail fare. My usual subject is "Me and My Stomach – Confessions of a Food Columnist". It always goes down very well.'

How a man who at dinner once at the Pedalows' could not tell the difference between Bœuf à la mode and Irish stew has the gall to set himself up as a gourmet is a mystery to me. Nor, as far as I am aware, do his literary tastes extend much beyond Hammond Innes and Lady Antonia Fraser.

'I never realized you were an expert on Rossetti,' I said pointedly.

'To tell you the truth,' he said, 'until this morning, I'd always thought he was a singer. However, the lecture agency sounded pretty desperate when they rang, and I thought: What the hell, it's only Leeds, and it's sixty quid and no questions asked. So I looked the fellow up in the encyclopaedia, invented a lurid love life for him and hurried off to King's Cross Station. The chairman said it was one of the best talks they've had all year. In fact they've booked me for a return visit in the spring.'

He then announced that he had a matter of some delicacy he wished to discuss with me. Naturally, I assumed he was referring to the incident in the Botticelli Restaurant. But nothing could have been further from his mind.

'The thing is,' he said, 'I've been asked to lecture for a week on a Mediterranean cruise. "Roman Provincial Life in the First Century AD". It's five hundred quid all found, plus expenses. The only problem is what to do about Percy – you know, my budgerigar. You couldn't possibly have him, could you? I think you owe me a favour.'

I was astounded at his impertinence and said that in my book it was he who owed a favour to me; but it was like water off a duck's back. Anyway, I've said I'll think about it. It won't do him any harm at all to sweat it out for a bit.

## Wednesday, September 28th

Morning spent wrestling with the problem of Hugh's budgerigar. I cannot imagine anything worse than having to share a room with a noisy cage bird. On the other hand, it's not as though I'm being asked to sit and talk with the creature, or take it out for drives in the country. A little added responsibility might be very good for me, and will, I feel sure, raise my stock in Victoria's eyes.

After lunch, put Hugh out of his misery by ringing him to say that if he really couldn't find anyone else to look after the budgie, I would be willing to take him on.

'Oh,' said Hugh, 'I never bothered to ask anyone else.'

## Thursday, September 29th

Am quite looking forward to my little visitor. I have made a space for him on top of the chest of drawers. I only hope he is not going to be messy.

## Friday, September 30th

Hugh dropped Percy off shortly after six. He seems a nice enough little chap, if not exactly bouncing with health.

'Ah,' said Hugh, when I mentioned it, 'that's because he hasn't been fed for a day or two. What with one thing and another, I haven't had a spare moment. I'm sure your local pet shop will oblige with a bag of seed. The large ones are more economical. Oh, and you might get him another cuttle-fish bone while you're about it. He becomes very bad-tempered if he doesn't get his cuttle-fish bone.'

It had never occurred to me they might have closed the pet shop in Holland Park Avenue. However, it really isn't all that long a walk up to Notting Hill Gate, and the chap there was very helpful, and most apologetic about being out of cuttle-fish bones. I sympathize with his comment that if he were a budgie he'd prefer a ladder and a mirror with a bell on it any day and can only hope that Percy sees it the same way. Arrived back at the flat to be confronted by Victoria demanding to know what the terrible noise was coming from my bedroom. I explained about Percy. 'If you ask me,' she said, 'keeping birds in cages is thoroughly inhumane, and I'm surprised at your agreeing to have anything to do with it.'

I see that he has already managed to break one of the rungs of his ladder. The super-strong model was certainly not worth the extra 25p, and I shall take it up with the pet-shop man next time I'm in.

# October

## Saturday, October 1st

Woken at the crack of dawn by Percy ringing his bell for all its worth. Under the circumstances, it is probably just as well that Jane, who sleeps in the next room to mine, is away for the weekend.

After breakfast, put my hand into the cage to remove the broken ladder only to receive a sharp peck from Percy that drew blood. I only hope that I have not caught one of those strange diseases that are occasionally transmitted from birds to human beings – like psittacosis. I certainly seem to be developing, for no very good reason that I can see, a very nasty sore throat, and I noticed tonight that my voice had become quite croaky.

## Sunday, October 2nd

To Kent early with Percy for lunch with mother. The moment I arrived I made a solemn pact with her not to discuss politics. She is convinced I am a socialist – which compared with her I suppose I am – and she blames me personally for the mishandling of the economy by the Labour Government in general, and for the smallness of her pension in particular. No matter how hard I control myself, it invariably ends in a shouting match. To my astonishment, the entire morning passed without a single reference to Mr Callaghan, and for once I was able to read the Sunday papers in peace. Was in the middle of a very interesting piece in one of the colour supplements when she came up behind my chair and asked what I was reading. I explained that it was an article about the French Resistance during the last war.

'How interesting,' she said, peering at the page. 'What's that photograph?'

I said that it was of a group of Resistance fighters in Clermont-Ferrand.

'Oh really?' she said. 'They look like a lot of lefties to me.'

By the time lunch was on the table, she had driven me into such a state of fury that I had completely lost my appetite. Matters were not helped by her saying at regular intervals, 'I do wish you wouldn't peck at your food, dear.'

Under the circumstances she could hardly have picked on a more unfortunate choice of phraseology. However, my throat was by that stage so sore that I could not have replied, even if I had wanted to.

As I was leaving mother said, 'I hope Percy's a good traveller.'

When I asked her why, through the agony of streptococci, she said, 'There's an awful smell in the car, as though someone has been sick.'

## Tuesday, October 4th

To dinner at Theresa Milne's. She is looking rather good for her age, I thought. She has just moved into a little house in Barnes and done it up very well. Philippe de Grande-Hauteville was there. I hardly knew him at Oxford, and yet I seem to bump into him everywhere. He has recently opened an antique shop in Notting Hill Gate, and I have promised to call in one day. He seems to me to be under the impression that I work for the BBC, I don't quite know why.

Sat next to a plain girl in beige who talked a great deal about people I had never heard of. I was giving her my views on the new Truffaut film when she suddenly interrupted me to ask if I wore false teeth, of all things.

I said that I did not, and she asked me if I was sure. I replied that I was positive, and asked her the reason for her question.

'Oh, nothing,' she said, 'it's just that you have a habit of doing something with your mouth that only people with false teeth do.'

I was quite taken aback and said that I hoped it wasn't something too off-putting.

'Not at all,' she said. 'In someone who doesn't have false teeth, it's really very charming.'

Why do I waste my time at such events?

## Wednesday, October 5th

A bizarre footnote to the Horse of the Year Show now taking place at Wembley. Vanessa's father, who is a psychiatrist, has had two patients in this week, complaining that they are unable to make love to their wives unless they have a bit in their mouths, and their wives are dressed in jodhpurs and spurs. I dread to think what goes on during the Motor Show.

## Thursday, October 6th

Percy seemed so depressed on his own in the bedroom this evening that I brought him through to the sitting room. Unfortunately he would insist on singing and chattering all through a TV programme we were trying to watch. Jackie said she thought having a pet around made the flat seem 'ever so cosy' and started feeding him pieces of apple. In the end, Beddoes became very cross indeed and said that one of these days he would strangle the bird with his bare hands. I wouldn't put it past him either.

## Friday, October 7th

An extraordinarily tiresome day one way and another. My scooter is on the blink again which meant travelling to work on the underground for the third day running. Then, during the lunch hour, I remembered that I had left a pair of shoes to be repaired at a little place round the corner. Went to pick them up only to find that the shoe-repair shop was now a sandwich bar. Took my place in the queue and when it came to my turn said that I had come to collect my brown suede casuals. The man cutting the sandwiches said, 'That's a new one on me, squire. Brown suede casuals. Would that be some sort of hamburger?'

I said that I hadn't got time for games and that I wanted my shoes back. In the end the fellow became rather insulting, so I left. On the pavement outside I found a policeman. I explained my problem and asked if he would be so kind as to help me get my shoes back.

'Shoes?' he said. 'From a sandwich bar?'

I sometimes think I would be far better off living in the country, if not abroad. Meanwhile I am short of a pair of brown suede shoes.

## Saturday, October 8th

A horrible shock. Lifted the cover off Percy to find him lying on the bottom of his cage, stone dead. He was in great form when I put him to bed last night. I suspect Beddoes had a hand in this – literally. My suspicions deepened yet further by the fact that when he finally got up just before lunch to mix himself a gin and tonic, he had a large plaster on his right finger. There was no point in beating about the bush, so I came right out with it and asked him how he had hurt his finger.

'If you must know,' he said, 'I cut it on that piece of broken glass from your Picasso poster which you left lying around in the kitchen.'

I still did not believe him and decided on a more direct approach still.

'You may be interested to know,' I said, 'that Percy is dead.'

'Oh, really?' he said. 'It must have been that smell in your car that did it. It's enough to finish anyone off.'

My real concern, though, was how to break the news to Bryant-Fenn when he calls to collect Percy tomorrow. In the end I decided that the kindest and simplest solution would be to replace him with an identical budgie. I therefore placed the dead bird in a large matchbox and carried him off to the pet shop where I was able to match him up with another bird so similar I would be prepared to give £100 to anyone who can prove that it isn't Percy sitting there in the cage.

## Sunday, October 9th

Have been reading the biography of Lord Curzon, and am most interested to learn that he married for money. This puts quite a different complexion on things. If a man like Curzon is prepared to be mercenary over such matters, then who am I to waste time with scruples? I have had quite enough of this shilly-shallying with Victoria and at the earliest opportunity shall invite her to join me for a weekend in Hertfordshire at Nigel and Priscilla's. They are always asking me why I don't bring a nice girl down. I sometimes think my sister and brother-in-law are under the impression I have no social life or friends at all.

Bryant-Fenn arrived after supper with a peeling nose and bright red forehead to collect Percy. He obviously did not have the slightest suspicion as to the budgie's real identity, and actually remarked on how well Percy was looking. It was more than I could say for him.

## Monday, October 10th

A beautiful, sunny day. Was just settling down over a cup of coffee with the new Barford development proposals when Bryant-Fenn rang to say that he was rather worried about Percy. When I asked him why, he said that he couldn't understand it: every morning for five years Percy had greeted him with the words 'Morning, cock, how's yourself?' but this morning he had peeled back the cover to absolute silence. He said, 'You haven't been messing about with him, have you? Frightening him or anything?'

Realizing that the truth was bound to emerge sooner or later, I said, 'Look, Hugh, I think I should tell you straight away that that is not Percy.'

'What do you mean, not Percy?' he said.

I said, 'I was going to ring you to explain. Percy died on Saturday. I didn't like to tell you last night and spoil your homecoming.'

'I see,' he said, 'so you decided to ruin this morning for me instead?'

'Well,' I said, 'you know what I mean.'

'Frankly,' he said, 'I don't. As I see it, this was a calculated attempt on your part to cover up Percy's death and deceive me into thinking that he was still alive and well. Well, if you want my opinion, it's the most underhand thing I have ever come across in all my life. Percy and I were extremely close – indeed he was in many ways my only real friend. If you'd just come right out with it and said, "Look here, Hugh, I'm afraid Percy has popped off," I would have quite understood. But to try and replace him with a second-rate double

31

is beyond all belief. Well, as far as I'm concerned, you can have him back, and the cage, too, for all I care. There's no way I could ever warm to him now.'

And he put the phone down on me. I have always suspected that beneath that cool, worldly exterior was a deeply hysterical human being.

Arrived home to find that he had already returned the budgie – cage, cover, spare seed and all. That's the last time I offer to help out.

Spoke to Victoria after dinner, who said she would like to come for the weekend to Nigel and Priscilla's at Bishop's Stortford, but it did not mean that anything had changed.

## Tuesday, October 11th

Left the office early on an urgent pretext and took the budgie back to the pet shop in the hope of getting my money back.

'What's wrong with him?' the owner asked.

I said that I was quite simply not satisfied with the bird. He asked me what sort of satisfaction I had been expecting. I said, 'Well for one thing, he doesn't say anything.'

He replied that if it was miracles I was looking for, I had come to the wrong place. I said that that much was obvious, adding that, in my opinion, pet shops in England are not what they were.

'Neither,' he said, 'are the customers.'

Rang the Joyces and spoke to Priscilla who said they would be delighted to have us for the coming weekend. I do hope Victoria is going to fit in to country life and will not be tempted to start any unpleasant arguments.

## Wednesday, October 12th

Is the whole world going mad?

I was driving to work this morning on my scooter when the driver of a Ford Cortina wound his window down and spat a piece of apple core straight into my lap.

'Excuse me,' I called out as we drew level at the traffic lights, 'that went on me.' He looked at me for a moment, threw the rest of his half-eaten apple at me, and drove off up the Bayswater Road. I was so busy trying to remember his number that I drove into the back of the car in front that was trying to turn right. As if I didn't have enough to worry about.

## Thursday, October 13

Life has become such a strain lately one way and another that I am seriously beginning to fear for my health. Just to be on the safe side, I have decided to go in for some of this Body Maintenance I keep reading about in the Sunday papers. I thought I might start off with something simple, like jogging in the park.

This evening a most extraordinary thing happened. At about six-thirty there was a ring on the front door. I opened it to find a black girl standing there, very tall, with the sort of hair that looks as though it has been ploughed. 'Hi, there,' she said. 'I'm Grace,' and marched straight past me into the flat. I said that I thought she must have come to the wrong address.

'Ralph does live here, doesn't he?' she said.

'Beddoes?' I said.

'Oh,' she said, 'is that his other name?'

Apparently Beddoes had picked her up on the underground on his way home from the office, invited her back to the flat and sent her on ahead while he went to get some cigarettes. She seemed a nice enough girl – a receptionist in a film company, she said. However, just to be on the safe side, I kept an eye on her till Beddoes returned.

'What do you think?' he said to me later in the kitchen, 'not bad for a choc ice, eh?'

One way and another I'm quite relieved to be going away for the weekend. Jane has very kindly agreed to look after the budgie.

## Friday, October 14th

To the office in my brown tweed suit. I usually wear it on Friday mornings, largely to annoy Armitage who is convinced that I spend every weekend as a guest at some grand country-house party. It must be terrible to be so full of envy. 'Off for another of your smart house parties?' he asked as I walked in.

'Oh, not really,' I told him casually. 'Just some friends in Hertfordshire. A spot of shooting tomorrow morning: a little *mah-jong* and dancing to a wind-up gramophone in the evening – you know the sort of thing.'

Happy to see his knuckles went quite white.

Picked Victoria up at her office at five-thirty and drove straight on down. Unfortunately have still been unable to get rid of the sick smell completely, so sprayed the inside of the car with liberal doses of Flowers of the Forest air freshener. We were sitting in a traffic jam in the Euston Road, when she said, 'If there's one thing I can't stand it's strong after-shave,' and wound the window right down. As a result, the whole effect of the air freshener was lost and by the time we got to Holloway Road, the sick smell was back again.

'I'm so sorry about the smell,' I said.

She said that she hadn't noticed it, but now that I came to mention it, it was absolutely filthy and did I mind if we opened *all* the windows? I was glad I had had the foresight to throw my old anorak into the back of the car at the last minute. Victoria said it was remarkably warm considering its age. Any fears that I might have had about her not fitting in with my sister and brother-in-law's rural way of life were dispelled the moment we arrived. I have never been very keen on that take-us-as-you-find-us attitude that appears to prevail amongst country folk, but Victoria seemed to take to it very happily. As we were unpacking the car I happened to make a comment to her on how funny Nigel's clothes looked after London.

'I don't know what you mean,' she said. 'I think he looks very well in them,' and to my surprise began to discuss sugar beet with him. From what I could gather, she seemed quite knowledgeable.

I felt Priscilla might have come up with something a little more appetizing than sausages for supper. They seemed a little high to my way of thinking, and the cauliflower was definitely over-cooked, but Victoria appeared to notice nothing wrong and even asked for a second helping of both.

I hoped they had not taken too much for granted over the sleeping arrangements and wondered if I should give some hint of the situation. However, Priscilla solved the problem very simply by saying, 'I've put Victoria in the big room at the end, and you're in the box room. I'm afraid the heating doesn't work in there, but you could always use your anorak as an extra blanket, if you want.'

'That's fine by me,' Victoria said with an enthusiasm that was quite uncalled for.

The box room certainly is very cold.

## Saturday, October 15th

Woke at nine with earache – presumably from driving all that way with the window down. Came down to find Victoria had gone out with Nigel in the Land-Rover to look round the farm. They seem to have hit it off surprisingly well.

A delicious breakfast completely ruined by James, aged six, who sat under the table, pulling at the hairs on my leg. I asked him to stop three times, but he took not the slightest notice and his mother said nothing to him, so eventually I leaned forward under the table and slapped him sharply on the wrist. He immediately screamed with rage and tried to bite me on the ankle.

I had expected Priscilla might have shown some sympathy. Instead she said, 'Would you kindly mind not hitting my child. It's very bad for children to be brought up in an atmosphere of violence.' I told her that was not *my* idea of bringing children up, at which she pointed out, rather unkindly I thought, that as I did not have any children I was hardly qualified to hold opinions on the subject.

At lunch (shepherd's pie and baked beans, which always give me terrible wind) Nigel suggested we might like to drive over to Braintree where some friends of theirs were having a clay-pigeon shoot. Victoria said she would love to, and I have always wanted to have a go at it myself. I went upstairs afterwards to change into something warm, but when I came down I found that Nigel and Victoria had already gone.

When I asked Priscilla why they hadn't waited for me, she said vaguely, 'Oh, I think they were under the impression you weren't very keen and had gone upstairs to read.'

In the evening, a small dinner party had been arranged in our honour.

'I think you'll like this other couple,' said Nigel. 'He's an architect, she writes. They're quite odd – well, that's to say, they're from London, too, so I expect you'll have a lot in common.'

In the event, it was a most successful evening, and we were

able to discuss a number of topics of interest to country folk – the decline in village life, the rights and wrongs of foxhunting, unemployment in agricultural communities, the preservation of the countryside and so on. It was all great fun.

Afterwards, when they had gone, Nigel said, 'I couldn't have kept all that up for much longer.'

'All what?' I asked him.

'All that chit-chat,' he said.

As I was getting into bed I caught my bad toenail on the sheet, tearing it painfully.

## Sunday, October 16th

Something very fishy was going on last night. Was so frozen by about three a.m. that I simply had to get up to look for a blanket. Not only was there a light showing under Victoria's door, but the door to Nigel's bedroom was slightly ajar. Yet I distinctly remember Priscilla telling me that they always slept with their door shut. I thought at first that he might have slipped downstairs for something, but there was no one down there when I looked, and no one in the bathroom either.

This morning Victoria did not come down for breakfast, and when she finally did appear, could not stop yawning. Neither, I noticed, could my brother-in-law. When I asked her if she had had a good night, she looked at Nigel, and said, 'A very good night indeed, thank you.'

I am not a suspicious man by nature, but I reckon there was a bit of fun and games going on somewhere.

After breakfast we all went to church. I am not, I'm ashamed to say, as regular a churchgoer as I might be, but I never fail to enjoy it when I do go, especially when the singing is good.

Evidently the Joyces' local church is not as well attended as some, and this morning's congregation consisted of eight elderly people who never opened their mouths from beginning to end. Under the circumstances one was hardly encouraged to 'Sing unto the Lord a new song'. Such singing as there was came from the so-called choir which consisted of a soft warbling from the district nurse, a growling basso profundo from the tiny gamekeeper who insisted on his own version of everything, and a piping tenor from Nigel who was largely off-key. The organist groped about somewhere in between. I heard Victoria make a half-hearted shot at the *Te Deum*, but she very quickly gave up the struggle. On the other hand, she gave a loud rendering of the General Confession, as well she might have.

Nigel read the first lesson – rather badly, I thought. He pronounced Micah as though it were Meecah. There was an embarrassing moment during the collection. Having anticipated a bag, it came as a bit of a shock to find that not only was it a brass plate, but that all the locals handed over their contributions in small brown envelopes. There was nothing for it but quickly to substitute the 10p piece I had ready for a pound note. I've enjoyed Mattins more, I must confess.

I was looking forward to a good, stiff walk after lunch, but Victoria said, 'Oh, I have to get back into town, I'm afraid.'

Having been brought up to believe that if you take a girl away for the weekend, it's your duty to bring her back again I had no alternative but to forgo my walk and drive back far earlier than I had expected.

Not surprisingly, we got caught in a bad traffic jam at Finsbury Park.

Whatever it was that Victoria had to get back for, it obviously was not very important, since she spent the entire evening in her bedroom.

All in all, though, I have a feeling I have made more progress with her than it may appear.

## Monday, October 17th

A glorious autumn day. Wore my brown tweed suit again to the office to annoy Armitage. Called in at MacFisheries en route to buy a brace of pheasant to take in with me. Unfortunately, the best they could offer was a couple of pigeons. I hung them nonchantly on the hat-stand in my office. When Armitage came in, he looked at them and said, 'Well, you obviously didn't have a very good weekend's sport. I could do better than that in Trafalgar Square with a catapult.'

## Tuesday, October 18th

Up at six, ready to start my jogging, but had hardly laced up my gym shoes when it started to rain, so returned to bed for another couple of hours of much-needed sleep.

## Wednesday, October 19th

Up at seven to find the day overcast but dry. Set off eagerly on my first morning of jogging. Am thinking in terms of buying a track suit and a new pair of gym shoes, but have decided to wait and see how it goes before involving myself in a lot of expense. Anyway, the split in the sole hardly noticed after a while. Had never realized before how lucky I am to have Holland Park on my doorstep. I could as easily have been in the depths of the country – although I was surprised to pass quite so many other joggers on the way. Everything went extremely well for the first ten minutes, although I was somewhat alarmed to discover that I was barely able to cover a hundred yards at a time without running out of breath. I also began to experience sharp pains in my chest. One hears all too often of young men dropping dead from heart attacks as a result of too much sudden exercise, so I stopped and rested on a bench for a while. Nearby was a stretch of grass surrounded by a low iron railing, and beyond it a path where a rather pretty girl was walking with a small white terrier. I stood up, ran forward and vaulted lightly over the railing. Foolishly, I caught my foot on the top and came down heavily on the damp grass, giving my knee a nasty bruise. I was lying there, dazed and winded, when the terrier suddenly took it into its head to attack me. However, its owner, instead of calling the nasty little brute off, merely laughed and walked on. The interesting thing is that, apart from experiencing a certain difficulty in walking, I feel 100 per cent fitter already.

## Thursday, October 20th

I would give a lot to know who it was who telephoned shortly after six o'clock this evening. I could hear the phone ringing as I was coming up the stairs. I hurried up the last two flights as best I could with my gammy leg and along the corridor. However, in my anxiety to extricate the front-door key from my inside pocket, I ricked my neck badly, and at the same time dropped the box of eggs I was carrying, breaking every one of them. I finally got the door open and had just reached the phone when it stopped ringing. I have rung up everyone I can think of, but none of them claims responsibility. Not only will my share of the telephone bill for this quarter be much larger than usual, but I am now incapable of moving my head without great pain. This will obviously put paid to my jogging for the time being.

## Friday, October 21st

At Armitage's suggestion, have decided to pay a visit to a sauna-and-massage place he knows of, just off the Edgware Road. I got the distinct impression that there is more to it than meets the eye, and I made quite sure he understood that I was not in the market for any hanky-panky.

'I don't know what you mean,' he said, all innocence.

He must take me for a complete fool. At all events, whatever they may or may not get up to in this particular massage parlour, it's bound to be an interesting experience, and my neck couldn't be more uncomfortable than it is now.

I have booked a three o'clock appointment tomorrow afternoon.

## Saturday, October 22nd

Hardly slept a wink last night for thinking of the massage parlour, and when I did, I kept having erotic dreams – one of which to my surprise involved Grace.

Arrived at the parlour in good time for my appointment. It all looked very respectable from the outside, with signs in the window for American Express and Access. I could not help reflecting what a strange world it is where you can even get pleasure on credit. Was surprised to find the receptionist was a man. He told me that I would be looked after by Michelle who was extremely capable. I said that it all sounded very satisfactory to me and that it would be a good opportunity for me to practise my French. At this he gave a little laugh, and called for Michelle through an intercom.

I was most interested to discover with what ease one slips into the demi-monde, and was beginning to feel quite at home when the door opened and in stepped a large, handsome young man with curly hair and a ring through one ear.

He was wearing white shorts, sandals and a T-shirt with the words I WANT TO GET MY HANDS ON YOU printed across the front.

The receptionist said, to my astonishment, 'Oh, there you are, Michel, this is Simon with a sore neck. It's the first time for him, so don't be too hard on him. I know how rough you can be.'

I remarked that I had expected the treatment to be performed by women.

'If you're looking for *that* sort of thing,' he said coyly, 'you've come to the wrong place.'

I decided the only thing to do under the circumstances was to play his game, so I said carelessly, 'Frankly, it doesn't matter to me one way or the other.'

He said that I was a devil, and hoped that whatever tensions I was suffering, Michel would be able to relieve them.

I followed Michel through some gaily coloured plastic strips into a sort of corridor with a number of doors leading into small booths. He showed me into the one at the far end and told me to take all my clothes off and lie face down on the couch. I heard him go into the next-door booth, where there was a lot of whispering, punctuated by laughter. I took everything off except my underpants and lay down as I had been told.

'I said *all* your clothes,' he said when he returned.

I remarked conversationally that he seemed to have a very good English accent. He said that, as he had been born and brought up in Cheltenham, that was hardly surprising.

When I was lying down again, he said, 'Is it just your neck that's giving you trouble, or do you require the full treatment?'

I had read enough of Beddoes's magazines to know what *that* meant, so I decided the best course would be to lay my cards on the table straight away. 'Now look here,' I said. 'I think I should tell you here and now that I am not that way inclined.'

'What a queer person you are,' he said, and started to massage my back.

I still can't make out whether he was having me on or not, but he certainly managed to put my neck right. I think the fact is, as soon as they realized they were dealing with a serious customer, they decided to play it straight, rather than risk any trouble.

All evening I noticed Grace kept giving me knowing sort of looks, as though in some funny way she knew where I had been in the afternoon. It wouldn't surprise me one little bit to discover she does a bit of that sort of thing on the side.

## Sunday, October 23rd

Was boiling myself an egg this morning in the kitchen when suddenly Grace rushed in wearing nothing but Beddoes's dressing gown, threw open the window and stuck her head out. For a moment I thought she was about to make some dramatic suicide bid, but she laughed and waved and even started cheering. I asked her what on earth was going on. 'It's Concorde,' she said. 'It always flies over at this time. I never miss it.'

I made some indifferent remark or other, at which she turned on me, her hands on her hips and her eyes flashing, and cried, 'But aren't you excited about it?'

I said that I was, quite.

'Well, I am,' she said, 'very. It's things like that that make me proud to be British.' And she marched off back to the bedroom.

It's extraordinary to think that someone like that should feel as responsible for the success of Concorde as I do.

While getting ready for bed this evening, I found that I have developed a nasty rash in a most awkward place.

No prizes for guessing where I picked that up from.

## Monday, October 24th

This morning's post brings a letter from the Lord Chancellor's department, summoning me for jury service on December 5th. This is very exciting news.

Beddoes, who, as far as I can see, has no social conscience whatever, tells me that according to someone he knows who's up in these things, anyone can get out of jury service simply by slipping the Clerk of the Court a five-pound note and muttering the word 'incontinence'. I shall certainly do no such thing. As the enclosed, self-explanatory leaflet points out, 'Jury service is one of the most responsible duties that the individual citizen can be called on to undertake.' I quite agree.

Apart from anything else, it is sure to be an interesting experience, and one of those things everyone should do once in their lives. Who knows, I might even find myself involved in a sensational murder trial, like that of the Krays, and have to be put up in a West End hotel and given police protection and goodness knows what else.

## Tuesday, October 25th

Am becoming increasingly concerned about this rash which shows no signs of clearing up.

Called round at the doctor's this evening after work, but he is obviously as baffled as I am. However, he prescribed some ointment, and said that it was probably just one of those things that go round from time to time.

I did not care for his implications one bit, but decided to let the matter drop rather than become involved in a long-winded explanation about my visit to the massage parlour and so on. It would almost certainly be misunderstood. I have long suspected that the majority of patients in his waiting room are there because they have been up to no good. In fact I have often seriously considered finding another doctor in a more respectable area.

## Thursday, October 27th

Great excitement. The Harrods Christmas Catalogue has arrived. I have never actually bought Christmas presents from the catalogue, or from Harrods, for that matter, but mother always sends it on, and I enjoy speculating on what I might buy in a moment of desperation: the man's sheepskin coat with the coyote collar at £475, perhaps? The President's Cocktail Hamper at £350? The Black 'Top Hat' Ice Bucket with bottle of Moët & Chandon Première Cuvée Champagne, magician's rabbit glove puppet and pack of trick cards, for a mere £17·50? Or possibly the jumping dolphin in clear crystal on chrome stand from Daum of France, signed, at £180? I simply cannot imagine how I have lasted all these years without one.

### Friday, October 28th

Rash showing no signs of improvement, despite the ointment. The doctor has finally admitted defeat and has made an appointment for me to see a specialist at the hospital on Tuesday week. I am beginning to wonder if I might not have contracted some rare skin condition that will set the entire medical world by its ears. Who knows, they might decide to name the complaint after me. Crisp's Disease. I can see the entry in the medical dictionary already.

### Sunday, October 30th

Now my toenail has come off completely.

### Monday, October 31st

A pink card arrived this morning from the hospital with an appointment to see a Dr Smithers. I only hope he is a little more *au fait* with his subject than my man.

A more immediate worry, though, is that it says on the bottom of the card: ON YOUR FIST VISIT [*sic*], PLEASE BRING A SPECIMEN OF URINE.

I have hunted high and low for a suitable container, but have been unable to come up with anything smaller than a 2 lb. Nescafé jar. What do other people do in similar circumstances? Frankly, I am rather stuck.

# November

### Tuesday, November 1st

The very mention of November for me conjures up images of leaves smouldering in London parks, roasting chestnuts over an open fire, and tea at the Ritz. Why this should be I cannot imagine, since I have never had tea at the Ritz in my life. Perhaps I should. It could be my next project.

The Pedalows have invited me to a firework party on Saturday. It seems rather short notice but have said I'll go.

### Wednesday, November 2nd

Grace has been showing increasing interest in the budgerigar, so tonight I asked her if she would like to have it. Her delight was positively childlike. Anyway, she has taken the bird home with her – to eat, I shouldn't wonder.

### Thursday, November 3rd

Armitage marched into my office this morning without so much as a by-your-leave and said, 'Oh, by the way, laddie. About the Barford project. They want suggestions on it in time for a meeting on Monday morning. I'd get my skates on if I were you.'

Who does he think he is?

### Friday, November 4th

This business of the specimen has been on my mind for some days now. I wonder if hospitals have any idea of the problems and worries they create for people when they make requests of this sort? In the end, called round at Fortnum and Mason during the lunch-hour and asked for the smallest pot of jam they had.

'What sort of jam did you have in mind, sir?' asked the assistant.

I told him the actual jam was immaterial; it was the jar I was interested in. Finally, after a certain amount of misunderstanding all round, we settled for a small pot of damson, one of the few jams I have never much cared for.

## Saturday, November 5th

To the Pedalows in Islington for the fireworks. It was all pretty much of a damp squib as far as I was concerned. Tim made a great fuss about a hot punch he had been working on all afternoon. He'd put far too much spice in it to my way of thinking and when no one was looking I tipped mine into a flower bed.

Philippe de Grande-Hauteville was there, and said, 'How's life at the BBC, then?'

I might as well talk to a brick wall as talk to him.

Also Theresa Milne, looking very old suddenly.

Hugh Bryant-Fenn much in evidence as usual, rushing about in a state of high excitement, letting off rockets in all directions and drawing everyone's attention to the ones he had bought. He made a particular fuss about a Catherine Wheel which he kept telling us cost him 85p. However, when it came to the point, the thing flew straight off the garden fence and into the compost heap where it fizzled pathetically for a second or two before going out. Thinking that was the end of it, I made my way towards the house, as did several others.

'Hang on,' we heard Tim shouting from the bottom of the garden. 'We haven't had the *pièce de résistance* yet. Everyone look at the flower bed.'

He then struck a match which he applied to a Roman Candle at one end of the bed. This duly went off, at the same time lighting a length of fuse which in turn lit another Roman Candle further along and so on. Everything seemed to be going according to plan, and everyone was congratulating Tim on his ingenuity when the fuse went out.

'Oh, hell,' Tim shouted, 'that's ruined the whole effect. It must be the damp. Will someone be an angel and light that next Roman Candle?'

Realizing that was the spot where I had ditched my drink, and not wishing him to discover the true cause of the failure, I volunteered and was just about to strike a match when the Candle went off in my face, scorching my forehead and completely burning off my eyebrows. Everyone was at once thrown into a frightful state. Vanessa became hysterical and had to be slapped round the face by the au pair girl. Tim kept trying to do a test he vaguely remembered from his Boy Scout days to check that I hadn't gone blind. Everybody agreed that I should see someone about it, so in the end Bryant-Fenn drove me down to the nearest hospital which by a curious coincidence was the very one I am due to go to about my rash. In fact I mentioned this to the nurse who took my particulars, but she didn't seem very interested. Casualty was full of people who had been injured by fireworks – many of whom had lost more than their eyebrows. I was all for going home after they had patched me up, but the doctor insisted on my staying in overnight, in case there was any damage to my eyes.

I was lent a pair of pyjamas and taken along to a men's surgical ward and put in a bed next to a chap who had just been operated on for impacted wisdom teeth. It was impossible to get a wink of sleep for the coughing, spitting and swearing that came from the next bed. It wasn't until four in the morning that I suddenly remembered that I was a subscriber to Private Patients Plan and could therefore afford a private room. I rang the night sister to explain this, but she was most unsympathetic and said that if I thought she was going to set to and move me at that hour of the night, I had another think coming, and that we'd all be getting up in another two hours anyway.

After she had left, the man opposite called out, 'I'd stay where you are if I were you, chief, and count yourself lucky. I knew a man in a private ward in a big London teaching hospital once who didn't get fed for two days.'

Spent the rest of the night composing a stiff letter to the PPP people cancelling my subscription.

## Sunday, November 6th

Beddoes arrived at visiting time bringing a huge plastic dahlia, a copy of *Spiritualist News* and an eyebrow pencil. Discharged finally at four.

No one in the flat. Struggled with the Barford project. Ate a boiled egg. Went to bed at nine.

I don't know which is more painful – my forehead or my rash.

## Monday, November 7th

If there's one thing I dislike more than men who carry hand-bags, it's men who wear make-up. However, in the circum-stances, it seems perfectly legitimate to imitate nature until my eyebrows grow again.

Everyone at the office showed great concern for my mis-fortune, and Sarah even went so far as to buy me a coffee from the machine at her own expense. Armitage, of course, had to make light of the matter by calling out, 'Hello, it's George Robey,' the moment I walked in.

I decided to sober him up straight away by discussing the Barford project. I left him in no doubt as to the amount of hard work I had devoted to the matter over the weekend in the face of considerable difficulty, and suggested that the sooner we got down to talking about the different ideas before the meeting the better.

He gave me a superior look and said airily, 'Oh, you can forget all about that. I talked it over with my uncle after lunch on Sunday, and we will probably go ahead with a plan based on my figures.'

## Tuesday, November 8th

To the hospital, carrying my specimen wrapped in a piece of Kleenex. Dr Smithers who examined me asked me a number of rather personal questions about my private life which under any other circumstances I should certainly have declined to answer. I am beginning to think all doctors these days have one-track minds.

Finally he said, 'In my opinion, you have got inter-**trigo.**'

This was exciting news. 'Really?' I said. 'What is that exactly?'

'It comes from two Latin words, basically,' he explained, 'inter and trigo. In fact, it's a heat rash.'

I suppose I should be relieved that it is nothing more serious, but I must confess to feeling somewhat disappointed. As I was leaving he said, 'That's a nasty burn you've got on your forehead. I should have it looked at if I were you.'

I was halfway home when I remembered I had forgotten to ask the nurse for my jam jar back, which is a great pity since it had a rather unusual label.

## Wednesday, November 9th

An unpleasant episode in the local grocer's. Called in on my way home from the office to buy a piece of their strong cheddar, and asked the girl if I could taste a small sliver first.

'Oh,' she replied sniffily, 'we don't allow that.' I said that in that case they were the only shop in London who didn't. But I might have been talking to half a pound of potatoes.

'Our cheddar is always very good,' she said. 'We always buy from the same people.'

I pointed out that it was not the quality of the cheese that was in question but the strength.

'Look,' she said, 'do you want a piece of this cheese or don't you?'

By now there was quite a queue building up behind me, so I replied calmly that I would take quarter of a pound. As she was weighing it out, I said, 'You see, if you had allowed me to taste it, I might have bought a much larger piece.'

'And if you hadn't liked it,' she said, 'you might have bought none at all.'

There is no arguing with people like that. It is a wonder to me they are still in business at all.

## Thursday, November 10th

For reasons that I cannot explain, I have become more and more convinced lately that I have been chosen as a subject for 'This is Your Life'. Indeed, every time I am summoned to Roundtree's office, I feel sure that Eamonn Andrews is going to step out from behind the filing cabinet clutching the book, and pronounce the famous words. And why not?

They often have people on that I have never heard of and the programme has been just as interesting as those featuring the famous, if not more so. My only worry is that they might take it into their heads to fly Eric over from Canada, and I still haven't paid him back the £25 I borrowed the Christmas before last.

## Friday, November 11th

Mike rang this morning to say that he was taking Victoria away for the weekend to stay with friends, and that he gathered I would be quite happy to have the children again. I asked him where he got that idea from.

'From Victoria, of course,' he said breezily.

## Saturday, November 12th

Mike arrived with the children at noon, drank half a bottle of my gin, and left with Victoria at one. Gerry much less pretty than I remember, and *much* more childish.

Could not face cooking lunch, so decided to take them to my local Greek restaurant for a kebab. Jane was hanging about in the sitting room, looking glum, so invited her along too.

During lunch I asked Gerry who the friends were that her father and Victoria had gone to stay with.

'What friends?' she said. 'As far as I know, they've simply gone for a dirty weekend at the Spread Eagle at Midhurst.'

I was so upset I was quite unable to finish my souvlakia. Tom was also making slow progress with his moussaka. When I asked him why, he said, 'It's your face. It puts me right off my food.'

After lunch Jane suggested a trip down the river to Greenwich. Drove to Westminster Pier and arrived just in time for the 2.30 boat. I cannot imagine how I can have lived in London all these years and not been on the river. It is simply fascinating and I cannot wait to go again. It was rather embarrassing that I was able to answer so few of the children's questions. However, Jane turned out to be a great authority on the subject, and pointed out all the buildings of historic interest that we passed.

At Greenwich we looked over the *Cutty Sark*, visited the Painted Hall, and climbed the hill to the Royal Observatory, with the children hanging on to Jane's every word. The afternoon was such a success that I bought everyone an ice cream before leaving and another upon disembarkation. There was one unfortunate moment in the car going home when Tom started complaining about the nasty smell in the car, whereupon Gerry announced that it made her feel sick, and then suddenly Tom was. It was a pity he couldn't have done it on the same spot as before.

After dinner Jane and I sat together on the settee with a bottle of Riesling and watched a play about a honeymoon couple renting a cottage. Whether it was the play, or the wine, I do not know, but before long I found myself putting my arm round Jane's shoulders as though it were the most natural thing in the world. One thing led to another, and before I knew what, we were in my room and in my bed. I know there is a fashionable trend among diarists these days to commit the most intimate details of their private lives to paper willy-nilly, and I am as well aware that sex sells books as the next man. However, as I made quite clear when I started my diary, I did not embark upon it with a view to publication nor has anything happened in the meantime to lead me to change my mind. What took place in my bedroom on the night of November 12th is a private matter between me and Jane. Suffice to say it was both successful and enjoyable.

## Sunday, November 13th

Woke up feeling even happier than I was yesterday, if such a thing were possible.

After breakfast, on a sudden wild impulse, I jumped up, threw open the window and shouted down into the street, 'A fiver for every man, woman and child who is happier than I am at this moment.'

A minute or two later there was a knock on the front door. It was Mrs Gurney from the flat downstairs.

'Aha,' I cried cheerfully, 'have you come to collect your prize?'

'I certainly have not,' she said. 'It may have escaped your notice, but today is Remembrance Sunday. If you must choose today for playing the fool, you might at least have had the decency not to do so in the middle of the two-minute silence.'

After lunch we all went for a long walk in Richmond Park. Any feelings I might have had for Geraldine have, I am delighted to say, disappeared completely, and my thoughts are now only for Jane.

I felt closer to her than ever this evening, and it came as a great disappointment when she said, 'I think I'll sleep in my own bed tonight, if you don't mind.'

When I asked her why, all she said was, 'I would rather.'

I lay awake for hours trying to work it out, and could only suppose I was suffering from a slight attack of bad breath. Eventually I got up and went to the bathroom and gave my teeth the scrubbing of their lives. When I got back into bed my gums were so sore I had to take a couple of aspirins to get to sleep.

## Monday, November 14th

Was able to get very little done in the office this morning for thinking about last night. I have decided that the bad breath was a red herring and that, as usual, female psychology lies at the bottom of this. Having submitted to me on Saturday night, she is now suffering from guilt, and is, quite under-standably, unable to face me.

Clearly the onus is now very much on me to put the situation to rights. Jane is a passionate girl, but at the same time obviously deeply inhibited. If I do not break down her inhibitions, no one will. It is unthinkable that she should finish up an old maid. My duty is clear, but not the way.

Against my better judgement, rang Beddoes at his office. I must say, for a successful City man, he always seems to have plenty of time to chat on the phone. I put the problem to him, as though it concerned someone in my office. He thought about it for a second or two and said, 'If I were you, I'd pay a visit to one of those sex shops. They've got all sorts of things for men with your problem.'

I said, 'There's nothing the matter with me,' but he just laughed and put the phone down. I shouldn't be at all surprised to learn that he has a problem himself. People who are forever trying to impute failure in others are frequently failures themselves.

## Tuesday, November 15th

Was in the Edgware Road at lunchtime today when I happened to find myself passing a sex shop. Unfortunately, I was already late for a luncheon appointment, otherwise I might well have investigated further.

## Wednesday, November 16th

Life is full of coincidence this week. Stepped off a bus in the Tottenham Court Road almost into the doorway of another of these sex shops. Purely out of curiosity, I decided to wander in and see what all the excitement is about. The middle of the shop was taken up by a book rack containing girlie magazines. I casually picked up one which had a picture on the cover of a girl with her hand down her knickers and went to riffle idly through it. However, this proved to be impossible owing to the plastic cover in which the magazine was firmly bound, and I was certainly not about to waste £1·50 on what would undoubtedly prove a great disappointment. There was also a rather unpleasant section containing more plastic-bound volumes with titles like *Pretty Boys* and *More of Bruce*. I doubt if that sort of thing would do much for Jane's confidence. On the other hand, what would?

The majority of the merchandise seemed to be aimed more towards the failed male than the unaroused female. I was particularly intrigued by a device called 'The Arab Strap' which claimed to combine 'visual pleasure with physical pleasure'. Since the effect of wearing the strap is to 'create a bigger bulge' the first part of the claim might conceivably be considered justifiable, but the second is surely so unlikely as to contravene the Trades Description Act? I took out my notebook with a view to jotting down the exact words when a voice behind me said, 'Can I help you?'

I turned to face a rather mousy girl with long straggly hair and no make-up, dressed in faded jeans and a cheese-cloth shirt, through which a pair of large breasts could clearly be seen.

I told her I wasn't there to buy anything; it was part of some research I was working on.

'That's what they all say,' she said and returned to the cash register.

I was certainly not going to give her the satisfaction of thinking she was right, and so continued calmly to examine the goods, making the occasional note as I went. Was on the point of leaving when I happened to notice a book on auto therapy. One is always reading about women tuning themselves up sexually with practices of this sort, and despite the plastic wrapper it looked a more serious work than most. £5·95 seems little enough to pay for a happy and successful love life. Unfortunately the girl was still on duty at the cash desk, and I had no alternative but to leave it till another day.

## Friday, November 18th

Returned to sex shop during lunch hour to find that a young man with a beard had now taken over. It is interesting how quickly one becomes accustomed to the most unfamiliar milieus, and it seemed the most natural thing in the world after paying for my book to stroll to the back of the shop where the sex films were being shown. It was rather like a public lavatory, with a narrow corridor and half a dozen doors leading off to either side. Men, many of them no older than me, were wandering from one to another as unselfconsciously as if it had been the Odeon, Leicester Square. There were three categories of film on offer: full length with talk, 2 × 50p; full length silent, 50p; and films in four sections, 10p per section. Not knowing quite what to expect, I decided to work myself in gently with 10p's worth. It was very dark in the booth, and I had a certain amount of difficulty in finding the slot for my coin, so that when the film started I was facing the wrong way, and by the time I had turned round, it had ended. I settled myself on the little wooden bench facing the white board on the back of the door before inserting any more money. The film appeared to be about two women on a bed, but the quality was so poor that I could not swear to this. When it ended, I could see that someone had written the word RUBBISH on the screen. Decided just for fun to try the booth next door which was showing *Hot Cheeks*. This concerned the activities of a man and two women on what looked very much like the same bed. Once again, the quality was so poor they appeared to be frolicking in a heavy rainstorm. However, just before the end there was a close-up of the man's face grimacing. I couldn't believe my eyes. It looked exactly like Beddoes. Before I had a chance to look more closely, the film ended. Discovering I had run out of 10p pieces, I hurried out into the shop to get some change, only to find that the bearded man had gone and his place had been taken by the girl again.

As I was leaving I heard her calling out, 'How's the research going then?' at which one or two of the customers turned and stared.

I ignored them all and hurried out into the street. It wouldn't surprise me to learn that Beddoes acts in blue movies; but how to find out for certain, that's the problem. One way or another I am going to find it very difficult to take him seriously from now on.

## Saturday, November 19th

Having left the book on auto therapy on Jane's bedside table, I was quite surprised not to have had any reaction from her as yet. I couldn't believe she hadn't noticed it. Finally, this evening, I mentioned the matter.

'Oh,' she said, 'it was you, was it? Whatever made you think I would be interested in a subject like that?'

'Like what?' I said, pretending innocence.

'Car maintenance for relieving tension.'

Beddoes came in later with Grace, but I simply could not bring myself to look at him.

## Sunday, November 20th

I see in the Sunday papers that someone has come up with yet more evidence about the fate of the Tsar of Russia and his family. Is Anna Anderson really the Grand Duchess Anastasia? The great debate continues. Oddly enough, I have always felt there was some doubt about my own origins. Every time I fill out a form for a new driving licence or a passport, I feel instinctively I should be putting something in the space marked *Title*. But what?

Until someone can come up with a satisfactory explanation as to why I am four inches taller than every other member of my family, I shall never feel entirely at ease in society.

'Oddly enough, I have always felt there was some doubt about my own origins.'

## Monday, November 21st

To Ryman's at lunchtime to buy a proper diary. Finally chose something plain and simple, and why not? I am neither a gardener nor a sex maniac, nor an aficionado of any of the curious pursuits for which most diarists seem to cater nowadays. If there was such a thing as a Diarist's Diary, I suppose I might be tempted to buy it, but there isn't. *Tant mieux.*

## Tuesday, November 22nd

My suspicions of Beddoes grow daily. The more I learn of him the more I am inclined to think that he is totally lacking in any moral sense whatsoever. Today he blithely admitted to me that he buys brand-new gramophone records, records them on his cassette machine, then takes them back to the shop claiming that they are scratched or in some way faulty, and gets his money back. A man who will do that will do anything.

## Thursday, November 24th

Thanksgiving Day. Not that I have a lot to give thanks for. Not only has Armitage been appointed Assistant Group Head, which effectively puts him over my head, but I now hear that Mike Pritchard is to move into the flat to live with Victoria. Why is it that *I* seem to be the only one to raise objections? The next thing we know we'll have Terry from Covent Garden bringing his strange friends back here, not to say daily raids by the Special Branch. I cannot think what I ever saw in Victoria.

Beddoes appears to have booted Grace out and taken up with a surly looking French girl by the name of Marie-France. She looks the sort who might act in blue movies.

## Friday, November 25th

Mike moved in this evening. I suppose it *is* more sensible for me to have Victoria's single bed in return for my double. As things stand with Jane, I do not seem to have much use for it at present. I hadn't realized Victoria's bed was quite so narrow, though. How they are going to fit the children in as well when they come tomorrow, I dread to think.

Fortunately, Jane has asked me down to her parents' at Oxted for the weekend which is a surprise, to say the least. There must be something behind it, but what?

## Saturday, November 26th

On the way down in the car, I asked Jane the real reason for her not wanting to sleep with me on Sunday night.

'I told you,' she said. 'I didn't feel like it. Don't keep on.'

Is it any wonder that I do not know where I am from one minute to the next?

Her parents live in a modest, mock-Tudor house with a small garden on the outskirts of the town. They welcomed me in a most friendly way and showed me up to the spare room which seemed very comfortable and had a Russell Flint reproduction over the bed.

Jane's brother Roland arrived just before lunch. He is a lively fellow, if a little bumptious, with an amusing line in Irish jokes. I gather he is training to be an accountant.

We had steak and kidney pie for lunch and vegetables from the garden.

Mr Baker seems to be under the impression that I work in Public Relations. I tried to put him straight there, but he said, 'Public Relations, marketing, advertising, show business, they're one and the same thing as far as I am concerned.'

Roland kept up a steady flow of chaff and sexual innuendo which was rather embarrassing, but all Mrs Baker said was, 'Eat up your stewed apples, Roland. They're fresh from the garden.'

In the afternoon we went for a walk on Limpsfield Common. There was very nearly an unpleasant incident when we were mocked by a group of village boys. Things could have turned very ugly, but I quickly took the wind out of their sails by pretending to have a crippled leg, and they soon lost interest and drifted away.

In the evening we all played Scrabble. I was unlucky to draw quite so many poor letters, and came last in every game except one. Mr Baker said, 'I always thought you PR chaps fancied yourselves as masters of the written word,' and went off to watch 'Match of the Day'.

Read for a while in bed, thinking that Jane would pop in and say good night. Finally, after half an hour, got up and made my way along the corridor to her room. I knocked on the door and was on the point of opening it when Mrs Baker stepped out of the bathroom and said, 'Now, now, none of your London morals in this house if you don't mind.'

I doubt if I have ever been more embarrassed in my life.

## Sunday, November 27th

A dull, overcast day. Spent the morning reading the *Sunday Express*. At noon we all drove up to the golf club for a drink. We went in my car. It was rather a squash, and the clutch started slipping slightly halfway up East Hill, but luckily it was only a short journey.

As we were climbing out, I heard Mrs Baker saying to her husband under her breath, 'I thought there was rather a peculiar smell in there, didn't you?'

Later, standing in the bar with our drinks, I remarked casually, 'Is it just me, or is there rather a funny smell in here?'

Mr Baker said, 'No, it's just you.' Everyone roared, but I think I'd made my point.

We had leg of lamb for lunch, with mint sauce made from fresh mint from the garden, and stewed plums and custard to follow.

At teatime Mrs Baker said, 'I expect we'll be seeing quite a lot of you from now on.'

This was news to me.

After tea Jane said that we ought to be getting back to town.

Roland said, 'Oh, I couldn't possibly bum a lift off you, could I?' I had rather hoped to have Jane to myself for once but was hardly in a position to refuse. I am not averse to giving anyone a lift, but even the best Irish jokes wear thin after a while, especially with a slipping clutch. I suppose he means well enough, but he's not what I'd call good brother-in-law material.

## Monday, November 28th

This evening Jane suddenly announced, apropos of nothing, that it was ridiculous for a man of my age and position to be driving around in a clapped-out VW. I said I had never held with the middle-class idea that a man should be judged by the car he drives. In my book, if a chap doesn't like you for what you are, he's probably not worth knowing anyway.

Jane said that she was not suggesting that I should rush out that instant and buy myself a Maserati. However, she did think it was high time I got myself something with a bit more poke to it. I laughed and said that I had heard of cars being thought of as sex substitutes, but that was surely going a bit far. She replied sharply that I knew exactly what she meant, and while I was about it, I could buy myself some new shoes.

'If there's one thing that puts me right off,' she said, 'it's suede shoes. Especially ones that look like dead animals.'

I said that they were a perfectly good pair of suede shoes and had been hand-made.

'Who by?' she said. 'The Lincolnshire Poacher?'

She then added that unless I bought myself a decent car and a new pair of shoes she would not be coming out with me again. I was tempted to point out that she had not been *out* with me for over a week. However, I am still very fond of her, and do not wish to upset the apple cart at this early stage. I suppose I had better go through the motions.

## Tuesday, November 29th

To the Haymarket Theatre to see the much-acclaimed revival of Ibsen's *Rosmersholm*. During the first act I turned to murmur something to Jane and was astonished to receive a sharp blow to the back of the head – delivered presumably by whoever was occupying the seat behind me. What does one do at such moments? I simply continued to watch the play as though nothing had happened. At the interval, turned round to find the entire row behind me occupied by very old ladies. I am mystified.

## Wednesday, November 30th

Noted two possible cars in the *Evening Standard*, but both had gone by the time I called. It's a mystery to me that anyone has the time to get to Sidcup at such short notice. Anyway, it's probably a blessing in disguise. Vehicles that are offered for sale privately always sound in far better condition than they really are.

# December

## Thursday, December 1st

Spent most of the morning scouring *Exchange and Mart*. However, my time has not been entirely wasted since I think I may have found just the thing. A Jaguar XJ6 – 1971 – for only £1300. Was surprised to find that what looked like a private telephone number turned out to be that of a garage in Tooting. However, Mr Woolcott to whom I spoke sounded very nice and not at all like a second-hand-car salesman, so I asked him honestly if he thought it was really worth my while trekking all that way out for a look. He said that he would be the last person to pull the wool over my eyes, but that if I wanted his honest opinion, I'd do well to get down there as soon as possible.

He has promised to hold it for me till six-thirty. He also said he would be prepared to consider taking my VW in part-exchange. One somehow does not expect to meet people like him in the second-hand-car trade. I was putting the phone down when I realised that Armitage was standing in the doorway watching me. 'Hello, Crisp,' he said. 'Frittering away the family profits on extra-mural activities again, I see.'

I said that if he really wanted to know, *they* had called *me*.

'It's not the cost of the call I worry about,' he said, 'it's the cost of your time. Do I gather you're thinking of buying a new car?'

I said that I was, if it was any business of his.

He said, 'In that case, may I give you a word of advice? Pay cash. They love cash, these car boys. Doesn't show in the books, see?' He winked broadly. 'My mechanic, a marvellous little Pole in Parson's Green, never takes anything but cash.'

'Mostly yours, it seems,' I said.

'Look, laddie,' he said, 'you can hardly expect to run a Natchford Special without spending a few bob on it from time to time.'

Really, for a so-called 'marketing man', Armitage is remarkably gullible.

'Now then,' he said, 'let's assume this heap of yours is worth a hundred at rock bottom. Thirteen hundred c.c. is it?'

'Twelve hundred, in fact,' I said.

'Yes,' he said, 'well there's nothing in it at that age. Sixty-two registration, you said. MOT?'

I told him eleven months.

'Eleven?' he exclaimed. 'Well, I mean, that's worth fifty quid in anyone's language. If I were you, I'd ask for £175 and settle for £140. Better still, how much is this thing you're thinking of buying?'

I said thirteen hundred pounds.

'Right then,' he said. 'If there's any trouble, offer him your car and a thou in cash, no questions asked. Tell him you'll bring it round in a suitcase. He'll probably waver for a bit and let you have it for ten-fifty. He'll be glad to have it off his hands.'

I was, I must admit, rather impressed at Armitage's know-how, and quite touched by his concern to get me the best possible deal, and thanked him very much indeed.

'That's all right, laddie,' he said. 'Any time. Oh, by the way, try not to use the phone on private business or we'll have to start docking your salary.'

Then, just as he was leaving, he looked down at the new shoes I had just bought and said, 'You might buy yourself a decent pair of shoes, too, while you're about it.'

He should talk!


## Friday, December 2nd

After work, picked up Jane from her office and drove down to Tooting. Unfortunately, my new shoes have started pinching rather painfully, and what with that and the slipping clutch, we made rather slower progress than I had anticipated.

At one point we were overtaken by a cyclist. I was sorry Jane did not see the funny side of it.

Mr Woolcott was even more elegant than I had imagined. And so, too, was the Jaguar. The paint and chrome-work were in excellent condition, and despite its J registration it had done only 45 000 miles. Mr Woolcott took us for a short spin in it, and it seemed to handle very nicely. I asked if I could take the wheel, but he explained that would be impossible because of the insurance arrangements. I thought I could detect a slight knocking noise in second gear, which was accentuated when turning left, but he said it was nothing to worry about.

When we got back, I said that all now rested upon how much he was prepared to give me for my Beetle. I thought he might have devoted a little more attention to it than he did, but he obviously realized it had been well looked after, and when I mentioned the eleven months' MOT, he said, 'Oh, really?'

I was rather nervous he might wish to drive the car and thus discover the slipping clutch. At one point he made as if to open the front door. The handle has a tendency to stick sometimes and I hurried forward to open it for him. He stuck his head in, but all he said was, 'What a funny smell.'

I decided we had shilly-shallied for long enough, and asked him what he thought.

He said, 'I've seen worse. Fifteen quid.'

I was astounded, and pointed out that the tyres were worth more than that.

He said he was very sorry; he would have liked to make it twenty, but not in that condition.

'Look,' I said confidentially, 'supposing I were to come round tomorrow with a suitcaseful of notes. What would you say to a thousand nicker for the Jag, no questions asked, and you take my car?'

'Frankly,' he said, 'we're not really interested in cash these days. We far prefer customers to make use of finance. That way we get a kick-back from the hire-purchase company. Now, do you want the vehicle or don't you?'

I told him I'd think about it and walked firmly away.

It's hard enough for a chap to keep his end up with girls nowadays as it is without being insulted by second-hand-car salesmen.

Arrived back at the car to find my door handle had stuck. I tugged at it several times without success, and then, just as I thought I was getting somewhere, it came away in my hand.

Mike, Victoria, the children and Beddoes are all away for the weekend, which I suppose is some consolation.

## Saturday, December 3rd

Was woken at eight this morning by Armitage, of all people, wanting to know how it had gone with the car. I told him it hadn't, and that I had obviously struck too hard a bargain. He sounded rather pleased at the news and said that his little Pole in Parson's Green knew a couple of chaps in Wimbledon who'd got a Cortina for sale.

'I've seen it myself,' he said, 'and I'd say it's a very nice motor indeed. It's got quite a bit of poke for its age.'

(I do wish people would stop using this expression. It quite sets my teeth on edge.)

There had to be a catch in it somewhere. 'How much are they asking for it?' I said.

'They're prepared to let this one go for three hundred,' he said.

When I asked him why, he said, 'Look, laddie. Don't ask too many questions. You're a friend of mine. Let's just leave it at that, shall we? The boys are on their way round to your place now. Good luck.' And with that he hung up.

Good luck?

It seemed a curious thing to say under the circumstances; and what did he mean by the boys? He made them sound like gangsters. At that moment there was a ring at the front door. I opened it to a small man in dark glasses and a pork-pie hat, smoking a small cigar.

'You the gent who wants to see the Cortina?' he said.

I decided that since he was there I might as well take a look, and, quickly throwing on a pair of trousers and a jacket over my pyjamas, I followed him downstairs.

The car was parked a few yards away down the street. It was bright green. As we approached, two big men in overcoats eased themselves out from the front seat. Just to show willing I looked the car over. I asked what year it was.

'Sixty-nine,' said Pork Pie.

I said I was surprised there wasn't more rust on it.

Pork Pie said, 'Fancy a little ride in it, do you, squire?'

I said that I didn't think that would be necessary, but that if they insisted, I wouldn't mind going just down to the end of the road and back. The two big men got into the front and Pork Pie and I sat in the back. We shot away from the kerb with such force that I was hurled back against the seat.

'Good acceleration,' I said with a laugh. We took the roundabout at the end of the road at about forty-five, but then to my surprise, instead of going right round and back again, we turned off and headed towards Hammersmith.

'I think you may have taken the wrong road,' I said.

'Harry knows what he's doing,' said Pork Pie, 'don't you, Harry?'

Harry nodded silently.

I suddenly felt convinced that I was being kidnapped. Any day now a ransom note made up of words cut out of a newspaper would arrive on mother's breakfast table in Kent demanding a vast sum for my safe return.

'I was hoping to borrow the money for the car from my mother,' I said casually, 'but she's even poorer than I am.'

'Oh,' said Pork Pie, 'we're not asking all that much.'

How much then? I wondered. Just a few hundred pounds perhaps. But was it worth it? And how humiliating if mother refused to pay. It was then that the thought occurred to me that all this was just an excuse to get me out of the way, and that meanwhile the rest of the gang were busy beating up Jane and doing the flat. I decided it was time for a showdown.

'Look here,' I said. 'I think I should tell you; I know what your game is.'

'Game?' said Pork Pie. 'What game would that be, then?'

'Well,' I said, playing it cool, 'you're trying to persuade me to buy this car, aren't you? Or am I very much mistaken?'

'Look,' said Pork Pie, 'we never try to persuade anyone to do anything against their will. If you don't want the vehicle, you only have to say so.'

I said that actually I had been thinking more in terms of a Jaguar.

Pork Pie said, 'A pity you didn't tell us that in the first place. Home, Harry.'

I decided to get out while the going was good, so I told Pork Pie that if it was all the same to him, I'd get out there, since I could do with a walk.

'Yes,' said Harry. 'Off a short pier preferably.'

I got out and they drove off at high speed towards the river.

The door to the flat showed no signs of having been forced, and Jane was still fast asleep. I spent a good half-hour going through all my things, but everything seemed to be in order.

Had planned to go down to Chelsea in the afternoon to look for a pair of trousers. However, under the circumstances, I thought it was wiser to stay indoors for the rest of the day, which was probably just as well, as it gave me an excellent opportunity to wash a few shirts.

Still no indication from Jane that she is interested in resuming our affair, which ended in such mysterious circumstances. I suppose it is up to me to make the next move, but not if it means further humiliation.

## Sunday, December 4th

According to Beddoes there is to be a New Year's Eve party in the flat, starting at ten and going on till dawn. This is the first I have heard of it. I cannot imagine a less pleasant way to start 1978 than prancing around in a silly hat with Beddoes's drunken city friends, Mike Pritchard and Victoria and her lefty lot – and being kissed by a lot of people I don't know and don't wish to know. I am certainly not in the market for any of that sort of malarkey, and I made myself clear on that point straightaway. Needless to say, this did not go down at all well, but then nothing I say ever does.

Victoria got up and left the room in silence. Pritchard poured himself another large whisky and soda and grunted incomprehensibly. Beddoes said, 'Typical,' and lit one of his beastly small cigars. Only the French girl, Marie-France, had the grace to keep her counsel. Not that she ever speaks to me anyway. Or to anybody else, as far as I can see. Still, I have more important things to think about than surly Frenchwomen – namely, my duties as a juror which begin at nine tomorrow morning. I shall need my wits about me.

Early bed.

## Monday, December 5th

My first day of jury service.

I drew up outside the court a good ten minutes earlier than requested only to discover they did not provide parking facilities as I had supposed. This meant driving around the neighbouring streets at the height of the rush hour looking for a free meter. As a result, I was five minutes late reporting for duty. To my astonishment, some two hundred people had also been called as jurors, and there was such a crush in the large courtroom in which we were assembled to be given our instructions that I had to stand in the doorway, thus missing much of what was said. Eventually, after much confusion and a good deal of sitting about in a smoke-filled waiting room, the jury to which I was assigned was summoned to its courtroom.

As soon as twelve of our number had been picked, the oath-taking began. The juror next to me, a coloured chap, was about to take the oath when he was asked by the judge what his religion was. 'Methodist,' he replied firmly. I was glad I was not asked to make a similar affirmation in open court since, although officially I have been a member of the Church of England all my life, I have recently begun to harbour certain doubts and have found myself leaning more and more towards Reincarnation. Only the other day I was in the British Museum buying some postcards when I found myself irresistibly drawn towards the Egyptian Room, a part of the building I have hitherto never felt the slightest desire to visit.

Once the formalities were over, counsel for the prosecution gave his opening address. The case concerned the handling of stolen property, and from what I could gather, things were looking far from rosy for the wretched-looking fellow in the dock. At all events, it was most interesting, and I was looking forward keenly to the parry and thrust of cross-examination when the judge announced that an important crown witness had failed to turn up and consequently we were dismissed until the following morning.

Jane came home early, very excited, wanting to hear all about it. I pointed out that her curiosity was entirely understandable, but that unfortunately it would be quite out of the question for me to divulge information that might prove prejudicial to the cause of justice.

'Oh, come off it,' she said laughing, 'that doesn't apply to me.'

I said that I was afraid it was impossible to make any exceptions, to which she replied that I was a pompous twit and marched out, taking my evening newspaper with her.

I wonder if Lord Widgery has to put up with this sort of behaviour every day from his friends? Incidentally, I am surprised that no mention has been made so far about appointing a foreman of the jury. However, I daresay a natural leader will emerge in time.

## Tuesday, December 6th

No sooner had we gathered in the jury room this morning than one of the women members announced, 'Well, as far as I'm concerned, I'm ready to cast my vote here and now.'

When I asked her what on earth she meant by this astonishing remark, she replied, as cool as a cucumber, 'It's obvious. Any fool can see he's as guilty as all get out.'

I reminded her in no uncertain terms that in this country a man is innocent until proven guilty, and that since all we had been given thus far were the barest outlines of the prosecution's case, we were hardly in a position to draw any conclusions.

'That's quite sufficient for me,' she replied crisply, and began to unwrap a packet of sandwiches.

I was reflecting that, were I by any chance to be appointed foreman of the jury, she would certainly be feeling the rough side of my tongue, when we were called into court and informed that, since yet another key witness had failed to materialize, the case would have to be held over and that consequently we were discharged.

A great disappointment, I must say, but the way things were going in the jury room, probably just as well.

## Wednesday, December 7th

Was woken shortly after seven this morning by an insulting telephone call.

'Hello,' said the man's voice. 'You're a fruit.'

I may not be up in all the modern jargon, but I have been around long enough to know that the word 'fruit' is a euphemism for a pansy. Naturally, I was pretty angry, and made my feelings known.

'I don't know who you are or what you are on about,' the man said, 'but I am trying to ring a company called Euro-fruit.'

'In that case,' I told him, 'you have the wrong number,' and slammed the receiver back on to the cradle with such force that I damaged the mechanism and it has been out of order ever since.

I have asked for an engineer to call round and repair it, but whether anything will come of it is anybody's guess. It is incidents of this sort that make one doubt the wisdom of our ever joining the Common Market.

## Thursday, December 8th

Finding myself alone in the sitting room this evening with Marie-France, I attempted to converse with her in French. I would not go so far as to claim that my command of the language is total. However, I have spent several holidays there – in Paris mainly – and can certainly make myself understood when I want.

'*Bonsoir*,' I said conversationally. '*Comment ça va?*'

She looked up from the French newspaper she was reading, shrugged and went on reading. I decided to try a more rewarding line of approach.

'*J'aime beaucoup le France*,' I said, giving a particularly authentic roll of the 'r'.

She looked up again, frowned and said, 'Huh?'

I said: '*Je disais que j'aime le France.*'

She continued to stare at me in blank incomprehension, and then suddenly her face lit up. 'Ah!' she exclaimed. '*Vous aimez* la France!'

I am not surprised Beddoes never speaks to her if this is what he has to go through every time he opens his mouth. It is certainly the last time I shall try. My doubts about the Common Market increase daily.

## Saturday, December 10th

Am completely stuck for a Christmas present for mother this year. She did mention something about a Burmese kitten, of all things. Out of curiosity called in at the pet shop in Notting Hill Gate and enquired if they happened to have such a thing as a Burmese kitten in stock. The man, who obviously did not recognize me, said he knew where he could lay his hands on one, and that they were £50 each. I may have to think again.

## Sunday, December 11th

Pritchard and Victoria set off early for a Vintage Car Rally in Basingstoke, leaving me with the children yet again. Jane and I decided to give Tom a treat by inviting the Pedalow children over for lunch.

We had my favourite: roast lamb with roast potatoes and Brussels sprouts, followed by caramel-flavoured Instant Whip.

The Pedalows arrived at twelve-thirty with Justin and Emma, and a friend of Emma's called Natalie who, the moment Tim and Vanessa had gone, began to behave in an atrocious manner, shouting, running in and out of the bedrooms, and bossing the other children about in a most unattractive way. She also had a streaming cold.

Lunch went off rather badly, thanks to Natalie. The lamb was very slightly underdone, just the way I like it, but Natalie announced that she was not in the habit of eating raw meat and threw hers on the floor. She then sulked.

I wouldn't have minded that, had it not been for her constantly running nose which made me feel quite sick. Unfortunately, Jane had made only enough Instant Whip for the six of us, so I had to forgo mine in favour of Natalie who took two mouthfuls and announced she didn't like it.

I would have finished it off myself but did not want to risk catching a heavy cold.

What a terrible thing it must be to have a child who is both plain and bad mannered. It makes me more determined than ever to think twice before bringing children into the world.

Mike and Victoria's outing was evidently not a great

success since they are now on non-speaking terms. A pity the same cannot be said about the children.

## Monday, December 12th

To Hyde Park for a stroll during lunch hour. Paused to watch a group of small boys enjoying an improvised game of soccer. One wild shot came in my direction, so I thought I would make myself useful by kicking the ball back to them. Obviously there is some special way of kicking a football that has to be learned. All I know is that I stubbed my toe so badly that I have been in considerable pain ever since.

It would have to be my bad toe, of course.

Curious how often I find myself thinking about that Instant Whip. I suppose it has to do with my horror of waste, so in that sense it is perfectly understandable. Pritchard moved out this evening, thank goodness. Now perhaps I can get my own bed back and enjoy a decent night's sleep for the first time in weeks.

## Tuesday, December 13th

In the middle of a meeting with the Barford client, I began to feel that unmistakable dryness at the back of the throat that presages a cold. I might just as well have eaten the Instant Whip after all. Home early and straight to bed with a glass of hot lemon and honey and the *Radio Times* for company.

Mother rang later to say that since she had heard nothing to the contrary, she presumed I would be going to her for Christmas as usual. But I was feeling far too ill to bend my mind to such trivial domestic concerns and told her I would confirm my plans as soon as I felt up to making decisions. In fact, I shall almost certainly be doing as she said. Christmas for me has always meant a time of peace and love and understanding, all three of which are sadly lacking in the flat this evening. For one thing, I still have not got my bed back.

## Wednesday, December 14th

Woke exhausted after a perfectly dreadful night. Throat like a raging furnace. Jane has been the only one of my so-called flat mates to show the slightest concern for me, bringing me hot tea and aspirins, and generally cossetting me like a baby. What a wonderful wife she will make someone. Possibly me.

Spent most of the afternoon changing the beds round, slightly ricking my back in the process. But at least I can now be ill in comfort. Not that I would have expected Victoria to understand. That's socialism for you.

## Thursday, December 15th

Cold taking its usual course. The sore throat has faded away to be replaced by a streaming nose and thumping head, both of which I infinitely prefer. Leafing through a pile of women's magazines which Jane very kindly left by my bed, I came across a most interesting article on Prince Charles and his girlfriends. He is quoted as saying how difficult it is for him, since every time he takes a girl out for the evening, he finds himself wondering if she would make the right sort of wife. I know just how he feels, and am only sorry we are not able to get together and talk this over as one bachelor to another.

What an extraordinary accident birth is. I could so easily have been born to the Queen in Buckingham Palace, and Prince Charles to my mother in Ashford General Hospital – had I not been conceived six and a half years earlier, that is. All in all, though, I am glad it turned out the way it did.

## Friday, December 16th

Rather than run the risk of passing my cold on to everyone else at the office, I have decided to delay my return until Monday morning. Despite my natural anxiety about how they are coping with the workload in my absence, I managed to enjoy a quiet, ruminative morning and afternoon. One so rarely has the opportunity these days to sit and think about things – particularly with Beddoes walking round the flat with a handkerchief tied round his nose and mouth, humming the theme tune from 'Dr Kildare'. It was quite funny the first time, but even the best of jokes wear thin after a while.

The only person for whom it does not, apparently, is Marie-France, who bursts out shrieking every time he appears. But then, of course, the French are renowned for their cruel sense of humour. I have a feeling he only keeps it up for her benefit; although I must say, a man who has to resort to facetiousness to keep his girlfriend sweet must be pretty desperate.

## Saturday, December 17th

Feeling 100 per cent better and dressed for the first time in nearly four days. Finally finished reading *Vanity Fair*. I have always suspected that Thackeray is a thoroughly overrated writer, and now I am even more convinced of it than ever.

## Sunday, December 18th

To bed with Jane tonight for only the second time since that marvellous weekend with the children, though why she should have picked on tonight to revive our affair I cannot imagine. I have always thought of Sunday evening as a time for reading, washing one's hair and going to bed early in order to be fresh for Monday morning, and had rather assumed she did too. Whether it was this, or the debilitating effects of my cold, I do not know, but the fact is it was not a success.

However, like the understanding girl she is, she said she didn't mind, and that it was probably just as well as she still had not read *The Sunday Times* colour magazine.

## Monday, December 19th

Was in the bath shortly before seven this evening when there was a ring at the front door. Since I was alone in the flat I jumped out, threw a towel round my waist and hurried along the passage. I opened the door to be confronted by three small boys who broke into a feeble ragged version of 'We Wish You a Merry Christmas' before seizing their noses and collapsing into helpless giggles. I told them I could see nothing funny in making a mockery of Christmas, and that if they wanted to get a penny out of me, they'd be well advised first, to get to know a few real carols, and second, to learn to sing. Needless to say, they ignored my advice completely and ran off down the corridor shouting 'Silly old git' and making rude gestures.

So incensed was I at their insolent behaviour that I set off down the corridor after them, meaning to give them a good box round the ears. Unfortunately, silly Miss Weedon from the flat next door had to choose that moment to emerge with Poppy, her loathsome snuffling pug, all done up in a woolly jacket. Instead of encouraging me in my efforts, she shouted, 'People like you ought to be locked up.'

I stopped and turned towards her in an attempt to explain the situation, whereupon she shrieked, 'Don't you try any of your tricks on me. Get back to the jungle where you belong.' And, snatching up the ghastly Poppy, she slammed the door on me.

I returned along the corridor only to discover that meanwhile my own door had closed and I had locked myself out, which meant trudging all the way downstairs and across the yard at the back to borrow a spare key from Gidney. At this rate I shouldn't be surprised if I have double pneumonia by Christmas Day. Not a very auspicious start to the festive season. Not only may I now have to start thinking in terms of moving, but in the neighbourhood I live in, I wouldn't put it past boys like that to make life extremely uncomfortable for me.

Indeed, as I was getting into my car later, they emerged from the block of flats next door, saw me, and began whispering and giggling together. I don't suppose they would go so far as to let my tyres down or bend my aerial. However, just to be on the safe side, when I returned, I took care to park several streets away. I have also taped up the inside of the letter box.

## Tuesday, December 20th

At lunchtime I popped round to the nearest charity card shop to buy my usual packet of six cards to send off to people who send cards to me. The worrying thing is that, with less than a week to go to Christmas, I have so far received only one card – from my local wine merchant. I only hope that friends who are planning to send me cards will not leave it much longer, otherwise it will be too late for me to send my cards back in time. Meanwhile I have sent off a card to the wine merchant.

## *Wednesday, December 21st*

My postman has become unusually civil of late despite delivering no mail to us. However, if he supposes that his ingratiating behaviour is going to earn him a Christmas box, he is sadly mistaken. This time last year, I slipped him a pound note with the compliments of the season and came home a few days later to find a large flat packet lying bent double on the hall floor. On it were printed the words: GRAMOPHONE RECORDS DO NOT BEND, underneath which was scribbled, 'Oh yes they do'.

## *Thursday, December 22nd*

Still no cards and, more astonishingly, not a single invitation to a Christmas party of any sort. I can perfectly understand firms cutting back on this sort of thing, but surely one's friends are not so hard-up that they cannot afford to offer one a glass of wine over the festive season? I would ask a few people in myself if only I could trust my flat mates to behave. I was lamenting this dismal state of affairs to Iversen in the office when Jane rang to say we had been asked to a dinner party this evening by some rather grand friends of hers who live behind Harrods.

My first reaction was to refuse. We were obviously asked only because some other couple had dropped out at the last minute, and in my book it never pays to be too readily available.

However, Jane insisted. Apparently she and the wife were at school together. Theresa Milne was there, looking rather pretty for once. Apart from her, the party turned out to be even worse than I had feared. The conversation was either about the City or skiing, in neither of which subjects do I have the slightest interest.

I attempted to introduce a little cultural relief into the proceedings at one stage by mentioning that I had just been reading the new John Fowles novel, and saying how astutely he had pin-pointed the Englishman's oppressive sense of guilt. But they all looked at me as though I were mad. I thought for a moment that the husband of Jane's friend was going to take me up on it. He lowered half a glass of brandy, looked at the others and said, 'Sounds pretty *foul* to me!'

Everyone roared like lunatics and helped themselves to more drinks. Unfortunately, neither Jane nor I had come out with our watches, and the evening dragged interminably. Finally, I could stand it no longer, and giving a great yawn, announced it was way past our bedtime and apologized for outstaying our welcome. Our hostess uttered the usual polite protests, and Jane said she did not want to break up the party; but I was adamant.

Naturally, I imagined that our fellow guests would take the hint and follow our example, but they made no attempt to move, and one or two of them even began to refill their glasses yet again. One of the men called out, 'Hello, a couple of love birds, eh?' and laughed coarsely.

It was an unfortunate remark under the circumstances, and one which in my view deserved a cutting reply. However, I think my cold stare was probably just as effective.

When we got home, we found it was only ten o'clock. I could not help bursting out laughing, and I was only sorry Jane did not see the funny side of it too. Not only are we now not on speaking terms, but I have since discovered that at some point during the evening someone had bent my car aerial nearly double. So much for the season of good-will.


## Friday, December 23rd

To Selfridges at lunchtime to buy Jane a pair of slippers. Rather expensive, I thought, for what they were. Tried at the same time to find something for mother, but had an altercation with woman at glove counter and left in a rage before I had had a proper chance to look round. The cat is definitely out of the question. Other considerations apart, I do not much relish the prospect of driving down to Kent on Christmas Eve on roads solid with drunken drivers with a strange cat jumping about in the back. I may very well have to fall back on a Marks and Spencer voucher, like last year.

To the pub for a lunchtime Christmas drink with the people from the office. Everyone ordered much more expensive drinks than usual – double whiskies, crème de menthe on the rocks, and so on – on the assumption that Roundtree, as head of the department, would stand the round. However, just as it came to the moment to settle up,

**he** announced that he had an important phone call to make and disappeared into the crowd. By then everyone else was busy talking, and it was left to me to pay. No one appeared to notice, however, and when it came to the next round, Roundtree announced that we should all pay for ourselves. I could not help noticing that everyone immediately reverted to half-pints of bitter and small sherries. Even so, a great deal more drink was consumed than usual, and one or two people behaved rather badly. Felicity, Roundtree's secretary, passed out into a plate of shepherd's pie, and at one point I saw Armitage kissing Sarah Smith with a lighted cigar stuck in his mouth. She didn't seem to mind at all.

Arrived home at four, rather the worse for wear, to find a note from the postman pinned to the front door saying that he had tried on several occasions to deliver some letters, but had been unable to do so, due to a malfunction of the letter box.

Now I have to trudge off to some post office miles away to collect them. If I were not so concerned that some of them might be Christmas cards, I really do not think I would bother. It only shows how little interest the others take in the day-to-day running of the flat that none of them had even noticed my anti-hooligan precautions – let alone done anything about them.

I had seriously been looking forward to a festive drink with Jane in congenial surroundings, possibly over a meal, so I made no other arrangements for the evening. However, it was nearly eleven when she finally appeared, and when I asked her where she had been, she replied that she had been making up for time lost last night. I do not know quite what she meant by this nor was she prepared to elaborate further. At all events, her behaviour was certainly not what one expects from a friend, and I not only did not give her her slippers, but I also made no attempt to kiss her under the piece of mistletoe which I have hung above the front door.

Before going to bed, I removed the greetings label from the slippers and wrote out another one, substituting mother's name for Jane's.

## Saturday, December 24th

To the post office to collect the letters. To my surprise, found I had received cards from many more people than I had expected, including Nick and Warthog, the Pedalows, Buffy and Moo, Mr and Mrs Baker, and Nigel and Priscilla.

Fortunately I had my five remaining Oxfam cards with me, so I was able to send them off straight away. I am only sorry there was no time to reply to the rest.

Returned to the flat to find an envelope propped up on my bedside table. It was a Christmas card from Jane saying that she was sorry to have missed me and that she thought it was just as well Christmas had come along, as we both needed time to think things over. She may; I certainly don't.

Beddoes and Marie-France were still in bed, but Victoria was up and about looking rather pretty for once in a long brown dress. She was also a great deal more friendly than usual, and even insisted on dragging me under the mistletoe and giving me really quite a passionate kiss. I have no idea what it was all about, but I must admit that I set off for Kent feeling more optimistic about life than I have for many days.

Arrived shortly before lunch to find mother busy preparing her traditional table centre. The motif has been the same for as long as I can remember: a mirror surrounded by cotton wool, representing a lake in winter. On the lake there are a number of white swans and a red Indian in a canoe, and on the snow, polar bears, penguins, and several tiny Christmas trees flecked with white.

The sight of it never fails to bring a lump to my throat. I was surprised to see that as yet there was no sign in the sitting room of the Christmas tree, which I always enjoy decorating. When I mentioned this to mother, she said, 'Oh, that's all right. Nigel and Priscilla said they would bring one with them.'

This was the first time I had heard that they were spending Christmas with us. They have not done so in the past, and I made a pointed remark to this effect.

The really annoying thing was that I had left all their presents in London, thinking to hand them over when I next saw them. After lunch I had to drive over to Ashford to see what I could find.

Shops solid with pushing, sweating, last-minute shoppers. Why *will* people leave all their Christmas shopping to the last minute? After an anxious and exhausting hour and a half, I came away with a woolly hat for Priscilla, a Farmer's

Diary for Nigel, and a modelling kit of the *Golden Hind* for James.

Arrived back at the car to find a traffic warden standing there writing out a ticket. I explained that I had not parked but merely stopped there for a second to pick up some last-minute shopping for an elderly lady. But I might have saved my breath.

'That's what we call parking,' said the warden, putting the ticket in a plastic envelope and sticking it on to my windscreen.

I suggested that as it was Christmas, he might be a little bit Christian about it.

'I don't see why,' he said. 'I'm a Jew.'

I may pursue the matter further or I may not.

Was watching the circus on television after tea when I heard Priscilla and Nigel arriving. There seemed to be rather more commotion in the kitchen then usual, so I went out to discover a tiny Burmese kitten rushing around the floor after a piece of wrapping paper. I have never seen mother so happy and excited. I asked Priscilla how she had managed to bring it down in the car. She said: 'In a cat basket, of course.'

Fortunately, they had also remembered to bring a small Christmas tree.

Just before dinner, James crept up behind my chair and rammed a piece of holly into the back of my head. Everyone seemed to think it was a great joke. It's a pity they don't pay a bit more attention to him than they do to the kitten.

Had very much been looking forward to Midnight Mass. However, somebody had to stay behind and babysit, and my neck was still very sore.

Dozed off in front of the fire and woke up to find the kitten had made a mess in the corner of the room. Cleared up as best I could and went to bed feeling slightly sick.

## Sunday, December 25th

Woken at six-thirty by James jumping on top of me dressed in commando outfit and firing a noisy plastic machine gun. Tried to get back to sleep after booting him out but failed.

Exhausted by breakfast time.

Afterwards we opened the presents.

Mother seemed quite pleased with her slippers, but she is so besotted by the kitten that very little else seems to register with her. Thank goodness they fitted – which is more than could be said for the pyjamas which she had bought for me. Still, they are a very nice colour, and they're always very good about changing things at Marks and Spencer.

When I gave the Joyces their presents, Priscilla said, 'Oh, I'm afraid we haven't got anything for you. We thought we'd be seeing you at a later date.'

I said that was all right and that anyway my presents were really rather dull. James said, 'Yes, they are, aren't they?'

To church on my own. Congregation as thin as the singing.

I attempted to fill out 'Oh, Come All Ye Faithful', by singing the harmonies, which I happen to know; but as no one else joined in, it simply sounded as though I was out of tune.

Lunch, when it finally appeared on the table, was an unexpectedly jolly and touching occasion. After I had carved the turkey, Nigel stood up and made a rather moving little speech about the importance of family life. He then proposed a toast to mother who was so overcome she burst into tears all over the Brussels sprouts. It was a pity the turkey was quite so tough. I suppose one should be jolly thankful one has anything to eat at all when one thinks of all the starving millions the world over. On the other hand, no amount of thinking will make a tough turkey tender.

After we had eaten we pulled some crackers. Mine wouldn't pull properly, so I reached inside to pull the crack out and it went off unexpectedly, giving my finger a nasty little burn.

James became over-tired after tea and mother suggested that an early night might not go amiss. Personally I think that a hand firmly applied to the seat of his pants would be more effective and told Priscilla so. But all she said was, 'When you have your own children, you may do as you wish.'

I certainly shall. I know Christmas is supposed to be a time for children, but surely not *all day*?

In the evening I proposed a game of canasta, which Priscilla and I used to play a great deal when we were young.

Unfortunately, I drew some very bad cards, and was thus unable to support mother as much as I should have liked. It was really rather humiliating. But then I am used to being humiliated these days.

## Monday, December 26th

Came down this morning to find that the kitten had got hold of my new pyjamas which I had left, I thought safely, on top of the piano, and not only ripped the cellophane cover, but also torn a small hole in the material itself.

Nigel suggested that I should pretend to the people at Marks and Spencer that they were like that when I took them out of the bag. I shall certainly do no such thing.

All mother could say was, 'You didn't know any better at his age.'

I certainly do not remember going around making holes in people's brand-new pyjamas – or making messes wherever and whenever the mood took me.

I seriously wonder if this creature has not turned her mind. If so, there is no doubt in *my* mind who is responsible.

As they were leaving after tea, Nigel enquired idly after Victoria. I told him that it was all off. He seemed rather pleased, I thought. I am more certain than ever that the two of them got up to something that weekend.

## Tuesday, December 27th

Another day's holiday to make up for the one we missed on Sunday.

Mother is convinced that some old hunting prints which she has found in the attic are worth a lot of money. They are by someone called J. Herring Senior and to my way of thinking are completely without artistic merit. However, I have promised to take them in to Sotheby's when I get back to town. It will set her mind at rest.

## Wednesday, December 28th

Beddoes has now taken up with a Chinese girl, if you please. What's more, they appear to have spent Christmas together in the flat. In bed I shouldn't wonder. The whole place positively reeks of stale Chinese cooking, and the sink is piled high with dirty crocks. I simply do not know where to begin.

If this is what happens when two of them get busy, I

dread to think what the place will look like after Saturday night's party. I shall certainly make sure my bedroom door is locked. Jane is staying at Oxted till Saturday. As for Victoria's unexpected show of affection last week, I fear this must be put down to seasonal enthusiasm. She could not be more off-hand if she tried. Who cares? I have far better fish to fry.

## Thursday, December 29th

To dinner with Mollie Marsh-Gibbon. I have not seen her for months.

She is easily the cleverest woman I know; rude, witty and critical of everything and everyone. She claims to be sixty-five but does not look a day over fifty. When I last saw her, she said she was going to redecorate the whole house; but the only difference I can see is that she has stuck back the peeling wallpaper with stamp paper. Food as bizarre as ever: Heinz tomato soup from the tin, fish fingers and a whole Stilton. We drank some red Australian wine which she had found in a closing down sale in Kidderminster. She insisted that most people would not be able to distinguish it from claret. Most coal miners possibly. When I mentioned the J. Herring Senior prints she said, 'My word, you're in luck if they're the real thing. He was the foremost print maker of Victorian times and is very much sought after nowadays.' Had another look at them when I got home. On second thoughts, they are really rather charming.

## Friday, December 30th

Armitage finally condescended to ask me if I had a good Christmas. I replied that it had been very pleasant and quiet.

'Everyone always says that,' he said. 'Well, I'm glad to say that I had a very noisy Christmas. We all ate and drank so much we made ourselves quite ill.' I do not see that is anything to boast about.

Rang Sotheby's about the pictures. The man I spoke to in the prints department was polite, though less enthusiastic than I had expected. But then I was playing my cards pretty close to my chest, too. I said, 'I have some Victorian hunting prints I think you might be interested in.'

'Oh, yes?' he said.

'They're by J. Herring Senior,' I added.

There was no doubt that his attitude towards me altered dramatically at that moment. 'Of course,' he said, 'we should have to see them before making any promises.'

I said that I quite understood and asked him when would be a convenient time to bring them in.

'Oh, any time during the week,' he said. 'There's always someone here.' I pointed out that under the circumstances, I would naturally prefer the opinion of someone of experience.

'We are all experts here,' he said. I asked him if I needed an appointment. He said that would not be necessary and that if I'd just like to bring them along, any time. I checked my diary and suggested Monday morning at about eleven. He said that would be fine, and that any time would do. It all sounds most encouraging.

## Saturday, December 31st

The last day of the Old Year, and one on which far too many people in my view indulge in retrospect. I understand the temptation, but prefer to take the positive line myself and look forward to the year to come. But then, of course, I do have plenty to look forward to, not least of which is the possibility of making some real money at last with these pictures. Indeed the only black spot on the horizon when I rose this morning was this so-called New Year's Eve Party. Clearly I could not possibly remain in the flat, but where else was I to go?

By an extraordinary coincidence, Hugh Bryant-Fenn rang just before lunch to say that if I happened to be at a loose end he had asked a couple of girls round for the evening, and perhaps I'd care to help him out? I could think of several people I'd rather see the New Year in with than Hugh, but needs must, and I agreed to go.

Spent the morning with the New Year's Honours List. Delighted to see the England cricket captain has been recognized, and not before time. By an odd coincidence, he was up at Cambridge at the same time I was at Oxford. I'm surprised we've never met. On the whole, though, an uninspiring list of dull businessmen, flashy show-biz personalities, and civil servants whose names mean nothing to me. As for the new Companion of Honour, it's extraordinary to think that a Trades Union official should now have the right to put the same letters after his name as Kenneth Clark. From now on, I shall certainly not be making any special effort to have my name included.

Arrived at Bryant-Fenn's shortly after nine, as arranged, to find him sitting in an armchair staring disconsolately at a blank TV screen, and not a girl in sight. He explained that they had just rung to say that they had remembered they were expected at a fancy-dress party in Fulham, but might look in later. This was disappointing news, but I put a brave face on it and pointed out that there was a rather good film on the TV.

Hugh said: 'Actually, the TV's on the blink. I've rung the people, but they won't be able to send anyone to look at it till next Wednesday at the earliest.' I won't pretend this was not something of a body blow. However, knowing Hugh's expertise in the kitchen, I consoled myself with the prospect of an excellent dinner with some first-class wines, and said cheerfully, 'Never mind. After all, what's an old film compared with a good meal?'

Hugh said that he was very sorry but he had arranged with the girls that they would bring the food and there wasn't a thing in the house.

'We could go out to a restaurant,' he suggested, 'if you really wanted. But frankly it's a bit of a busman's holiday for me. On the other hand, there's an excellent Indo-Pak take-away round the corner. I could write it up for my column. You don't happen to have any money on you by any chance, do you?' I am perfectly prepared to admit that my taste in curries may not be shared by all, but I still do not see that was any reason for him to insist quite so firmly on the Prawn Biryani and the Tandoori Fish, especially as I thought I had made it quite clear that I'm not that keen on fish.

After dinner we played Monopoly, a game I have never much cared for and for which I must admit I have very little natural talent. I thought he behaved very selfishly in not selling me Liverpool Street Station when I already had the other three, and I was very unlucky to miss the chance of buying Park Lane and Mayfair.

At ten to twelve there was a ring at the front door. Hugh, thinking it was the girls, rushed to open it and I followed.

To our surprise it was two other girls, both extremely attractive, dressed in leather motor-cycling gear. We could not believe out good fortune.

'Can I help you?' Bryant-Fenn asked them in a rather obviously suggestive tone of voice.

'We was looking for Tony, actually,' one of them said.

'There must be some mistake,' Bryant-Fenn said. 'I'm Hugh.'

'So I see,' said the girl, and the two of them walked off down the stairs.

Hugh put the kettle on for coffee after that, and said he would tune in to the BBC on his transistor for Big Ben. I do not know if it was the curry or what, but I suddenly had to rush to the loo.

When I came out, Hugh said, 'You've been an age. The New Year's ten minutes old already.' This is the first time in over twenty years that I have missed seeing it in. Unable to face going back to the flat, so stayed the night on Bryant-Fenn's sofa, which is far from ideal for a full night's sleep. Not exactly a propitious start for the year ahead.

# January

### Sunday, January 1st

Awoke stiff and cold after an extremely uncomfortable night. Rice Krispies and instant coffee for breakfast. I am more convinced than ever that someone should expose Bryant-Fenn for the gastronomic fraud he is. Lunched alone off pork pie and Guinness at the Cricketers. Returned to the flat at four. Victoria and Jane still busy clearing up. Beddoes in bed, as usual. Rehearsing for another blue film, no doubt. Astounded to find my bedroom door open. Went in to discover my bed had been slept in and obscene anatomical additions made to my bullfighting poster. Although I immediately changed the sheets and took down the poster, I could not rid my mind of the feeling that I had been personally violated. Needless to say, neither of the girls claimed any knowledge of the incident, and when I mentioned the matter to Beddoes, all he said was, 'The trouble with you is that you're jealous.'

He seems to see everything in terms of sex. The thing that really concerns me is how anyone managed to get into my room in the first place. Someone obviously must have a spare key, and until I know who, I shall not feel at ease in this flat again. The only good thing to be said for the New Year so far is that I can at last start making my entries in a proper diary. Extraordinary how much more significant everything now appears.

### Monday, January 2nd

To the office by taxi. A great extravagance, but one has to be prepared to spend money if one wishes to make any, and I could not run the risk of the prints being ruined by a damaging scratch from a careless umbrella on the Underground. To Sotheby's for my eleven o'clock appointment. I was interested to note as I entered that there is to be a sale of prints later in the week, which no doubt explains their interest in mine. There were many more people waiting in the print department than I had expected. However, I went straight up to the desk and addressed myself to a young girl employee. 'I've come about the J. Herring Seniors,' I told her in a low voice. 'Someone is expecting me.'

She looked down at my brown paper parcel. 'May I see them?' she asked.

'I did ring yesterday,' I reminded her.

'If you'd just undo the parcel,' she said.

As I struggled with the Sellotape and tissue paper, I said that I supposed they had to ask customers to undo their own parcels just in case there was any question of damage. She did not reply but picked up one of the prints and ran her fingers lightly over the surface. Her colleague, a young man, looked across at her and gave her a knowing nod.

'I'm sorry,' she said, 'but I'm afraid it's a reproduction. Next, please.'

I was perfectly astounded and reminded her of the trouble and expense to which I had gone, entirely at the suggestion of her colleague. But all she said was, 'I'm sorry. Next, please.'

As I was wrapping up my rejected wares, I remarked casually that she might be interested to know that I had already been offered a not inconsiderable sum for them elsewhere. 'I doubt it,' she said, 'but if it's true, take it. They're quite worthless. Next, please.'

I suppose it is easy enough to make mistakes when you spend so much of your day looking at real rubbish. As I was leaving, for example, an old lady shuffled forward and produced from a worn shopping bag a small oil painting.

'A pound,' the girl told her.

'A pound?' squawked the old lady. 'A pound? But the frame alone is worth more than a pound.'

'Actually,' said the girl, 'if you must know, the frame is really rather nasty.'

It was all a bit pathetic.

## Tuesday, January 3rd

Jane seems very friendly all of a sudden, and tonight gave me some sprouts to go with my pork chop. Does this mean she wants to start up the affair again, and, if so, should I encourage her? I am not entirely convinced that she is the girl for me, and I do not want to lead her up the garden path.

How difficult these affairs of the heart are.

## Wednesday, January 4th

Beddoes said something extraordinary this evening. 'I find it helps if you refuse to answer a single thing a woman says to you for at least an hour after you come in in the evening.'

What can he mean? Since most of the women he takes up with do not speak a word of the language anyway, I cannot see that it makes the slightest difference whether he talks to them or not.

## Thursday, January 5th

Christie's are as unenthusiastic about the J. Herring Seniors as Sotheby's. I shall certainly seek a third opinion.

## Friday, January 6th

Twelfth Night. Sorry to say Bonham's even less interested in the prints than the other two. I am reluctant to admit defeat, but I do have better things to do with my lunch hour than travel round London being snubbed by art dealers.

After supper took down the Christmas decorations watched by Beddoes. He contributes less and less to flat life. I also have a sneaking suspicion he might be carrying on a secret liaison with Victoria, but have as yet no proof.

## Saturday, January 7th

Jane asked me down to Oxted with her for the weekend, but I declined the invitation. It won't do any harm to keep her guessing for a while longer.

An unfortunate incident in the greengrocer's. Was standing in a queue waiting for a cauliflower when Victoria appeared behind me. She said she wanted some carrots and onions for 'our' stew. As far as I know she has not seen Pritchard for some time, so she could only have been referring to herself and Beddoes. A black man was in front of me, buying a great number of oranges. He went out looking so depressed that I remarked to George on the fact.

'Yer,' said George. 'What you might called browned off.'

Naturally I roared, but Victoria was absolutely furious and accused George of racism, threatening to report him to the Race Relations Board and goodness knows what else. Not only did she slam the sitting-room door in my face this evening, but I obviously shan't be able to go into that shop again for a very long time.

## Sunday, January 8th

To Kent for the day to return the prints. When I broke the news to mother, she said, 'Oh, I knew they were reproductions. I thought it was worth a try, though.'

During tea she told me that the other night as she was leaving after drinks at the Scott-Percivals, Denys Ramsden, who must be eighty if he's a day, put his head through the car window and gave her a French kiss. I do not believe this story. Apart from anything else, I am certain mother would not recognize a French kiss if it was handed to her on a plate.

Something is definitely going to have to be done about that kitten. I was sitting reading the Sunday papers in the wing chair when the wretched creature suddenly launched itself off the top of the drinks cabinet straight on to the top of my head. When I tried to pull it off, it sank its claws and teeth into my hand and drew blood.

Mother seemed to think the whole incident a cause for great hilarity. I wonder more and more about her sanity.

## Monday, January 9th

It may be a little late in the day to start making New Year resolutions, but mine are none the less serious for that. I shall write them down to remind myself:

1. To make some money.
2. To think seriously about getting married – possibly to Jane, but ideally to someone with money.

3. To find somewhere else to live. I am getting too old for this type of flat life.

4. To move more freely in society. I am always reading in the diaries of the famous how they dined here and lunched there; sat next to this person at table and met that one at the theatre. I see no reason why I should not do the same. My problem is that my life is too often taken up with domestic trivialities, and I allow my time to be wasted by people of little worth and influence. I shall take steps to break out of this little world in which I have become trapped in recent months, and give far freer rein to my personality and talents.

## Wednesday, January 11th

Invited Jane to dine with me. Normally, I would have chosen a modest trattoria like San Frediano, or an amusing dive like Joe Allen. But now I feel I have reached a stage in my life when I should be aiming for quality in all things. A pair of hand-made shoes from Lobb's may cost three times more than a pair bought at Freeman, Hardy and Willis, but they last three times as long, if not longer. I realize this argument does not apply in quite the same way to food, but the principle is the same. One should not be afraid to spend money; the more one spends, the harder one is obliged to work to replace it. This is how successful people get on in life, and it is probably one of the main reasons why I have not. Expansion is the key word from now. I therefore ordered a table for two at what Hugh Bryant-Fenn tells me is the best restaurant in town, Le Gavroche in Lower Sloane Street.

Jane was clearly surprised at my choice, and rightly made more of an effort than usual with her appearance. The food was simply delicious, and the wine excellent. I am not sure it was quite worth £55, and it is not something I am planning on doing again for a while. But there is no doubt Jane's attitude towards me has changed dramatically, and although I have not gone so far as to resume our affair in the technical sense, I certainly left her in no doubt of my feelings, which I am happy to say are stronger than ever. It is extraordinary what a sense of confidence money gives one. I only wish I had more.

## Thursday, January 12th

I did not speak to Jane for at least an hour after coming in this evening, yet it does not seem to affect her feelings towards me one little bit. I have not felt more cheerful for years.

## Friday, January 13th

My attention has been drawn to a curious phenomenon of modern life. Nine out of every ten young people I pass in the street appear to be acquiring small bruises on the sides of their necks. When I mentioned this to Jane, she laughed and said, 'Well, what's so extraordinary about that? They're love bites. We always gave them to each other when we were young – didn't you?'

I replied that, as far as I knew, I had never bitten anyone on the neck, nor had anyone ever attempted to bite me. Jane said that it all added to the fun of love-making, and the trouble with me was that I was far too inhibited.

I do not understand what she can mean.

## Saturday, January 14th

To the theatre on my own to see this new sex show. Normally, I would not dream of going to such a thing, but I was interested to find out what all the fuss is about. After all, how on earth can one be expected to give one's opinion on important issues of the day unless one has had first-hand experience? Never having been to a sex show before, I was absolutely astounded by the whole thing. I had no idea that such things were said and done on the public stage in this country.

Indeed, on more than one occasion I was compelled to close my eyes, put my fingers in my ears and hum loudly in order to drown what was being said. And yet, in the interval, perfectly normal and respectable-looking people were walking about and chatting and smoking as though nothing whatsoever had happened. I can only suppose that there are many more devotees of this lewd form of entertainment than I had realized. I understand now how poor mother must have felt when she was staying with friends recently and unwittingly started reading a copy of *Penthouse* which she found on her bedside table.

As far as I am concerned, the only good thing about the evening was that I did not, as I had feared I would, come away with an inferiority complex about my private parts.

## Sunday, January 15th

Nor, I am glad to say, does it appear to have inhibited my sex drive, if last night's performance was anything to go by. I am more and more convinced that the basis for a happy marriage is a happy sex life.

On the other hand, I thought Jane's comments about my figure were rather uncalled for. She is far from perfect herself, but I do not draw attention to the fact. Besides, I have always understood that women like men to carry a little weight. Perhaps I am very old-fashioned.

## Monday, January 16th

Sarah in the office tells me she is on a diet that is so successful that she has lost five pounds in as many days. The essence of the regime, I gather, is fresh unsugared grapefruit with every meal.

Breakfast consists of half a grapefruit, followed by fried eggs and bacon and one cup of coffee without milk or sugar. Lunch is half a grapefruit followed by meat and green vegetables; dinner ditto. One cup of tea is allowed per day plus an optional glass of skimmed milk before going to bed. It sounds remarkably painless, and according to Sarah, really works. I shall start it tomorrow.

## Tuesday, January 17th

First day of my diet. Breakfast actually more substantial than usual.

Lunched at Italian bistro round the corner from the office. Half a grapefruit, a plain veal escalope, undressed green salad and coffee. Simply delicious.

Dinner very similar except for a small steak in place of the veal.

I feel better for it already.

## Wednesday, January 18th

Diet still going well. Surprised not to have lost any weight yet. However, bathroom scales notoriously inaccurate. Sarah says the headache is all the poison coming out, which strikes me as rather far-fetched.

Suggested to Beddoes that he might well consider trying the diet, too, since he has put on quite a bit of weight lately. But all he said was, 'People who think thin, think small.'

Is it my imagination, or is he losing his hair?

## Thursday, January 19th

Delighted to discover I am able to tighten my belt by one notch. Interested to note on the way to work just how many overweight people there are in London. They none of them look very happy to me.

Lunched with Barford client in smart new restaurant in Covent Garden.

Astounded to find they did not have grapefruit on the menu. It would not matter quite so much if my diet were not the sort that must be followed to the letter. Pointed out the omission to the waiter who said that he might be able to find me some grapefruit juice. I asked him if that would be sweetened or unsweetened, and he said he would enquire. He returned with the news that it was very slightly sweetened. I said that I was very sorry but that would be quite out of the question, and would he mind terribly if I slipped out and bought myself a grapefruit? He said that that was up to me, but that of course he would have to charge me skinnage.

The client chuckled at this, and I joined in with a rueful smile, but I really do not care for waiters who make jokes at the customer's expense.

Fortunately, there was a fruiterer's nearby and despite a short queue, I was back in no time at all.

Surprised to find on my return that the client had disappeared. The waiter handed me a note saying: 'Your guest left this for you.' Apparently he had remembered he had some urgent shopping to do, and although he was sorry not to have had a chance to hear my marketing strategy proposals, he felt sure they could wait until I was able to give the matter my wholehearted attention. He also wished me luck with my diet.

What a pleasure it is to work with such sympathetic people. If nothing else, our meeting has certainly been a great help in cementing client relations.

In the afternoon found I had developed a nasty tummy-ache. Sarah said, 'Perhaps you've got your belt done up too tight.' I said that it was far more likely to be the effect of my stomach contracting – an observation that was shown to be founded on fact when I stood on the bathroom scales this evening and discovered that I had lost no less than six pounds.

Beddoes pointed out that the scales had not been right ever since they had been used in a game at the New Year's Eve party. He may be telling the truth or he may not, but on balance I think I prefer to believe my own eyes than anything he tells me. (No joke intended.)

## Friday, January 20th

To my local barber's after work for my usual monthly trim only to discover the place completely empty, the windows covered in white paint, and a sign announcing: OPENING HERE SOON. KEBAB HOUSE. If his kitchen is half as dirty as his washbasins, we can expect a few gippy tummies around Holland Park from now on.

## Saturday, January 21st

Oddly enough, my own stomach is still none too settled. Am wondering if it is something I ate.

## Sunday, January 22nd

Find I really look forward to my egg-and-bacon breakfasts, despite attacks of indigestion that often follow. Tummy also slightly upset still.

Remarked on this to mother when I drove down for lunch. She said: 'I'm not surprised with all that grapefruit you eat. You're obviously suffering from too much acidity.' I'd rather suffer from an excess of acidity any day than an excess of Burmese cat, but said nothing.

Decided to make a spot check on the weight on mother's

bathroom scales. Incredible as it may seem, I found I was five pounds heavier than when I got up this morning. As I was leaving I remarked to mother *en passant* that her scales needed adjusting. She said, 'That's most unlikely considering I had them tested only two days ago.'

Who by, I wonder? Cyril Smith?

## Monday, January 23rd

To the office still feeling far from well.

Bumped into Armitage in the lift who said, 'You look terrible. You know your trouble, don't you? You're putting on weight. You ought to do some exercise.' Had a long talk with Jane this evening. I cannot remember a time when I was more pleased to see her. By no stretch of the imagination could she be described as an ornament to society, but I really believe I enjoy her company more than anyone I know. At least she does not spend all her time criticizing every move I make, like some people I know.

## Tuesday, January 24th

Have decided to give my diet a rest for a few days. A week is quite long enough, and despite the fact that the weighing machine at my local chemist's appears to concur with the one in mother's bathroom, I definitely *feel* thinner which is the main thing. It's a pity I don't feel better.

## Wednesday, January 25th

This morning at breakfast Jane said, 'Has anyone told you that you have blackheads on your nose?'

At first I thought I must have misheard her, but she repeated this extraordinary observation, adding that in her experience a good rub with a nail brush would not go amiss – and after all no one should know better than she about facial blemishes.

I did as she suggested, but unfortunately went rather too far and made the tip of my nose bleed so profusely that I had to go round all day with a small piece of cotton wool attached to it – a fact that did not go unremarked by Armitage, needless to say.

## Thursday, January 26th

This morning's post brings a sensational offer: the chance to buy a magnificent new book entitled *Wildlife in Britain* at £1·75 less than the normal price. I cannot imagine why I have been picked out of so many millions of householders to be the recipient of this remarkable offer, but clearly it is an opportunity not to be missed. 'Just think,' it says in the glossy leaflet, 'with the help of this magnificent volume you can now learn to identify pied wagtails in the Mall or lone buzzards in the Scottish Highlands!' The possibilities are endlessly fascinating. 'Why not plan exciting day-trips to explore your own ecological area? Experience the thrill of seeing a badger; catch a glimpse of the rare pine marten; watch a lone otter gambolling in a Hebridean stream; wonder at the strange barking of the muntjak.' And all of this for less than ten pounds.

I have always been very keen on wildlife, and although I do not manage to get out into the field as often as I would like, I always make a point of looking in at the nature programmes on TV. I shall certainly send off for the ten days' Free Examination straight away. I shall also say YES to my name being entered for the Great £50000 Holiday Wildlife Game. The first prize is a round-the-world trip for me and my family, or £7000 in cash. I know which I shall choose.

## Friday, January 27th

To the opera with Mollie Marsh-Gibbon. It is an art form for which I have never really acquired a taste, and second-rate productions of *Carmen* in English are hardly guaranteed to change my opinion.

To her flat for supper afterwards. Noticed the wallpaper has started to come away again. We ate cold chicken and tongue and potato salad with a bottle of English hock-style white wine which Mollie declared was barely distinguishable from the real thing. I am bound to say that there was something in what she said – although I wished I'd had the expertise to refute it. It is high time I started educating my palate.

Knowing Mollie's interest in the countryside, I mentioned

the wildlife book. She said, 'Sounds to me like yet another of those cockeyed schemes that are forever being dreamed up by seedy entrepreneurs to make money out of the idiot public by exploiting their desire for instant, potted knowledge. Anyone with a genuine interest in nature discovers what he wants by first-hand observation, not by flipping through the pages of books that are designed primarily to adorn the coffee tables of middle-class suburbia.'

It is always a mistake to reveal one's ignorance to Mollie, and if I do decide to find out more about wine, I shall certainly take care not to mention the fact in her presence.

## Saturday, January 28th

Last night I had the most extraordinary dream in the course of which Fiona Richmond lay naked in a huge plate of fried eggs and bacon. When I told Jane about this, she said that in her opinion there was nothing more boring than other people's dreams, and that anyway I should have been dreaming about her.

The point about it, which she clearly failed to grasp, is that it just goes to show the effect these sex shows can have on perfectly normal, well-balanced people without their realizing it.

## Monday, January 30th

I really feel I cannot allow this business of my nightmare to pass without making my feelings known to the proper authority. Devoted much of the morning to penning a pithy letter to the managing director of the company responsible for putting on the sex show, with copies to the producer and the cast. I pointed out that if a perfectly sane, well-balanced member of the audience could have his subconscious distorted in such a dramatic way, I dreaded to think how such an entertainment might affect those already mentally and sexually unhinged. I added that from a purely artistic point of view, the show had been well beneath the standard one expects from a West End show, and that I thought the least the management could do by way of recompense was to return my money. I sent it by recorded delivery. I shall be most interested to hear what they have to say.

# Tuesday, January 31st

No sign of my wildlife book as yet.

Was in the middle of washing up this evening when Jane suddenly announced that she felt our relationship was not getting anywhere.

I asked her where she thought it ought to be getting. She replied, 'I have no idea, but wherever it is, it quite obviously isn't getting there, is it?'

I said that, as I understood it, relationships were not supposed to *get* anywhere; they were meant to *be*. At this stage she accused me of trying to evade the issue, as usual, and before I knew what, I found myself involved in a quite unnecessary row. In an attempt to assure her of my affection, I stepped forward to embrace her. Unfortunately, our two pairs of spectacles became locked, with the result that when I pulled away from her, I dragged hers off her nose and into the sink, smashing both lenses and bending one of the side pieces.

I do see, it *is* rather annoying to have to go round for the next week or so in a pair of round black National Health frames, but I still do not think that is any reason to take quite such a strong line against me. We must all learn to take the rough with the smooth, and the fact that she is not prepared to be forgiving over a comparatively unimportant misfortune like this, does not bode well for our future married life together.

# February

## Wednesday, February 1st

Penelope's birthday. It will be eight years this summer since we decided we were not really meant for each other, yet I often think about her still. On an impulse, I decided to ring her, but found that the last number I had for her was the Queensgate flat. After much telephoning, I finally traced her whereabouts through Harry Jeavons, of all people, who told me that she had finally married an out-of-work sociologist and become self-sufficient in a converted ploughman's cottage near Barnstaple. Got through after lunch. Surprised to discover my heart gave a little jump at the sound of her voice, just as it always used to. She seemed genuinely pleased to hear from me again after all this time, and suggested I might like to drive down for lunch on Saturday.

I said that I thought it was rather a long way to come for lunch, but she said, 'In that case, why not stay the night? We've got plenty of room, as long as you don't expect the Savoy. I know Ben would really love to meet you.'

Oddly enough, I have been thinking more and more recently about the possibility of escaping the rat-race for a simpler, more wholesome existence in the country, and I shall be most interested to see how they have got on.

## Thursday, February 2nd

Still no sign of my wildlife book, but so looking forward to seeing Penelope again that scarcely anything else seems to matter. Refused coffee from the machine for the first time in four years. From now on I shall avoid touching food or drink that has not been made from natural products.

At lunchtime popped out to buy the Seymours' book on self-sufficiency. It makes fascinating reading. Am particularly interested in the section on the cow. They write: 'The cow should be absolutely central to the economy of a small-holding.' I could not agree more. Section on the pig less interesting.

Planted some mustard and cress in an old ice-cream container.

## Friday, February 3rd

Called in at my local grocer's on the way home to buy half a dozen eggs. When the girl produced them, I asked her if they were fresh.

'Fresh in yesterday,' she replied in an off-hand manner.

'I am not interested in the date you received them. It's the date they were laid that I need to know,' I said.

'How should I know when they were laid?' she replied. 'I'm a shop assistant, not a chicken farmer.'

I told her that there was no necessity to take that tone with me, and although it may not be a shop assistant's job to watch eggs being laid, it *was* her job to be civil to customers. I then asked her if they were farm eggs. 'Says so on the box,' she said with a shrug. 'Dairyfield Farm.'

I said that sounded like a made-up name if ever I had heard one, and reminded her that it is an offence against the Trade Descriptions Act to describe eggs as farm eggs if such is not the case.

'Here,' she said, 'are you some sort of policeman, or what?'

I said, 'Merely an ordinary member of the public who wants to know precisely what he is paying for.'

'If you ask me,' she said, 'you're making a lot of fuss over nothing. You asked me for six large eggs, and I gave you six large eggs. For all I know they may be ostrich eggs that have been interfered with by the head-shrinkers of Papua, but that's no concern of mine. Now, do you want them or don't you?'

I said not unless she could guarantee to me that they were real fresh farm eggs, adding for good measure that there were no ostriches in Papua. She simply put the eggs back on the shelf and walked away without so much as a word.

I could have pursued the matter with the manager, given the time and patience, but a quiet word with the Trades Description people will certainly prove very much more effective. I shouldn't be surprised if there isn't quite a stink about this.

No sign yet of my mustard and cress – or of my wildlife book.

## *Saturday, February 4th*

Made an early start for Barnstaple, but traffic terrible anyway. Is it any wonder people like Penelope and Ben opt out of modern society?

Finally drove in through the open gate and immediately ran over a chicken or, to be more precise, a cockerel. Apparently he was the very first creature they bought when they arrived. By way of consolation I remarked that they must have become used by now to sudden set-backs. Ben said: 'Yes, but not quite as sudden as that.'

Had for some reason pictured Penelope in a long, flowing patterned dress, looking very romantic and beautiful like Dorelia John, and was most disappointed when she appeared in the doorway in jeans and T-shirt looking rather fat and unwashed – just like every other girl one sees in London. Ben looked more the part, in his collarless shirt with sleeves rolled up to his biceps, his old army trousers tied up with string and his heavy brown boots. He might have stepped straight out of the pages of a novel by D. H. Lawrence. He also hadn't shaved, I noticed.

After a while they offered me a glass of their home-made wine which tasted exactly like mouldy vinegar.

Then the children came in to be introduced – Seth aged seven, Job five, and Amos three. Penelope said, 'It's about time you started a family.' I felt like saying, 'Not if they turn out to look anything like these.'

They all appeared to have the most extraordinary number of holes in their pullovers, and when I remarked on this fact, Ben said, 'They're meant to be like that. It's called open weave. We finished them only the other day on the hand loom.'

Penelope said, 'We thought they were rather successful.'

Ben added, 'And they cost only a fraction of the sort of thing you find in the shops.'

And look it, I thought.

Lunch took an extraordinarily long time to prepare so that it was difficult for me to refuse a second glass of their vinegary wine. It was unfortunate that they had chosen to make every single stick of furniture with their bare hands since there was not a single chair or bench that was remotely comfortable.

Needless to say, there was no gas or electricity; such heating as there was came from open wood fires, and lighting was all by oil lamps. I noticed there were only two bedrooms, but did not like to ask where I would be sleeping – in the stable no doubt with the three sheep, two goats, cow, donkey, pregnant white New Zealand doe rabbit, eight Khaki Campbells and as many Buff Orpingtons as had escaped the wheels of visitors' cars. Lunch appeared finally at 2.15 in a large, steaming casserole.

'How delicious,' I said. 'Chicken.'

'Yes,' said Penelope. 'To be precise, the one you ran over this morning. Nothing goes to waste here.'

Ben then produced a small jug of their home-made ale which tasted to me exactly the same as their wine. I hoped they might close the window while we ate, since there was a cold wind out and it was blowing straight down my neck. But when I drew Ben's attention to this, he said: 'You city people don't know what fresh air is. You'll soon get used to it.' I daresay I might have done had it not been for the appalling stench of manure that came in with it. It was so strong that at one point I really wondered if I was going to be able to finish what was on my plate.

When I mentioned Tim and Vanessa, whom Penelope had known, she said, 'We're different now, and there's no point in pretending we're not.'

After lunch Ben slaughtered one of the goats and Penelope sprayed the fruit trees with tar wash, some of which splashed on to my suede shoes, leaving a nasty mark. Later we had a cup of dried pea tea which seemed to me to taste no different from the wine and the beer. They seemed genuinely disappointed when I announced that I had suddenly remembered I had a lot of work to do in the morning and would therefore be unable to stay the night after all. However, I promised to return again in the summer and try some of the goat's-hoof jelly. As I drove out through the gate, I felt a strange bump under my rear wheel but decided not to stop.

## Sunday, February 5th

Got up late. Still tired after long drive yesterday. Weather cold and wet. Thank goodness I decided not to stay. Went into the kitchen and found someone had moved my mustard and cress. Hunted high and low all morning, but without success. Mentioned the matter to Beddoes when he finally appeared at tea time. He said, 'Oh, Birgit and I decided to have a tidy up yesterday and we threw it out with the rest of the rubbish. We wondered what it was.' When I asked him who Birgit was that she should take it upon herself to interfere with other people's property, he told me airily that she was 'a piece of Scandinavian tail' that he'd picked up on Aldgate East Underground station on Friday afternoon. I did not conceal my distaste at the crudeness of his language, and commented coldly that, as I understood it, he was going out with Victoria.

He said, 'Well, I'm not now, so there.'

While I am relieved to hear that Victoria has seen sense at last, the fact that some foreign girl whom I have never met, and never want to meet, should decide to throw away my mustard and cress is something which I can neither forgive nor forget. Thought about penning a note to the Trade Descriptions people re the eggs, but really I have better things to do with my time. Suddenly the winter seems very long indeed.

## Monday, February 6th

Despite a particularly unpleasant journey to work and the continuing non-appearance of wildlife book, I am happy to be back in civilization once more. Dr Johnson was right of course. 'A man who is tired of London *is* tired of life.' Self-sufficiency is for the bored and the boring, and I do not think anyone could accuse me of being either of those. Celebrated my return with two cups of coffee from the machine and felt rather sick for the rest of the morning.

## Tuesday, February 7th

With Jane to dinner at the Pedalows'. I quite agree, their little mews house is charming, but not as charming as all that. Tim was very full of his new BMW 528, and after coffee he took Jane for a quick spin in it. On the way home, Jane said, 'I do not understand why you cannot have a nice car like Tim's.'

I said, 'Because I do not happen to be a partner in a family stockbroking firm where a large expensive car goes with the job.' She replied that I always had an answer for everything, and I am afraid we had words about it. Frankly, the sooner I make some money the better for both our sakes, but I am certainly not going to tell her that.

## Wednesday, February 8th

This evening I asked Beddoes if he could ask around his influential City friends and see if he couldn't come up with a tip that would make me a shilling or two on the stock market. He said he was very sorry, he didn't have anything to do with that side of the business. What *does* he do? I'd like to know.

## Thursday, February 9th

Have decided to hand over my portfolio to Tim instead. He is very enthusiastic and says he has had a sniff of something that might turn out to be very interesting indeed, and will let me know in a couple of days.

## Friday, February 10th

Bought the *Financial Times* on the way into work. Looked up the share prices, but was quite unable to make head or tail of them. However, I daresay I will get the drift in time, and anyway the arts pages are excellent.

## Saturday, February 11th

My wildlife book has arrived at last and is every bit as fascinating as the leaflet suggested. I had no idea there were tawny owls in Regent's Park. I must remember to look out for them the next time I am up that way. Disappointed not to have heard any news of the Holiday Wildlife Game, but perhaps one should not expect more than one excitement in a day.

## Monday, February 13th

No news as yet about my investment. Rang Tim as soon as I got into the office. I gave my name to the secretary and she asked me to hang on for a moment. There was a brief silence and when she returned she said she was very sorry but Mr Pedalow had just gone out to a meeting and would not be back until late afternoon. I cannot explain why, but I had a funny feeling that she was not telling me the truth and that Tim was trying to avoid me. I had expected better treatment from a friend, and hope that he is not going to start acting the goat with me, otherwise I shall seriously have to think about removing my portfolio and entrusting it to someone who is prepared to take it more seriously.

## Tuesday, February 14th

Received a Valentine card of appalling sentimentality depicting a young couple walking hand in hand through a bluebell wood. The printed message inside read: GIVE ME YOUR HAND AND I WILL LEAD YOU TO PARADISE. Assuming this to be one of Beddoes's feeble jokes, I confronted him with it at breakfast saying that I might be desperate, but I wasn't as desperate as all that! Beddoes then made a coarse joke and we both roared and slapped our thighs. Then Victoria made an excellent joke to the effect that I should be very grateful that it had been *handed* to me on a plate, and we roared all the harder. Suddenly, to our surprise, Jane threw down her toast and marmalade, burst into floods of tears and rushed from the room slamming the door behind her. Naturally, I went after her and asked her what was the matter. 'If you must know,' she blubbed, 'I sent you that card, and what's more, I meant every word of it.' Oh dear, oh dear.

## Wednesday, February 15th

Tim rang to say he was planning to put me into Benganese Conglomerates, whatever they may be, and how much did I have in mind to invest? Obviously it is one of those very rare occurrences, a copper-bottomed certainty, so I decided to throw caution to the wind and plunge my entire savings

*'Then Victoria made an excellent joke . . .'*

of £500. As Onassis said in his biography, which I have recently been reading, if you want to make a lot, you've got to risk a lot – a philosophy that certainly paid off for him. On the other hand, of course, Onassis did not have to waste his time hoovering the sitting-room carpet and generally cleaning up other people's messes. I do not quite understand why I have been landed with this job, but I have.

## Thursday, February 16th

At the risk of tempting providence, I have decided to treat myself to a new suit: a blue double-breasted worsted, I thought, with a heavy pin stripe, in keeping with my new image as a man of affairs. However, despite visiting over half a dozen reputable men's outfitters in the West End, I am quite unable to find anything remotely approaching this. Where *do* people go nowadays if they want traditional off-the-peg tailoring?

## Friday, February 17th

Again bought the *Financial Times* to see how my shares are doing. But try as I might, I am quite unable to find anything that sounds like Benganese Conglomerates. Have I been taken for a ride? I have always had my doubts about Tim Pedalow.

## Saturday, February 18th

Spent all morning going round the shops but still unable to find the suit I want. In the end settled for a similar thing in plain dark grey worsted. I think it looks rather good on me. I only hope I shall be in a position to pay for it.

## Sunday, February 19th

To Regent's Park to try to catch a glimpse of these tawny owls I have been reading about in my wildlife book. But not an owl to be seen or heard. A most unproductive day in all respects. I do not know which disappoints me more: my wildlife book or Regent's Park. However, I am looking forward to wearing my new suit tomorrow.

## Monday, February 20th

Armitage most insulting about my suit. Said I looked as though I had stepped straight out of the Munich crisis and that the pre-war look might go down very well amongst my country friends, but it was not the sort of image the firm wished its young executives to project. I said that in my opinion – and I was not alone in this – there is a correct way for business people to dress and an incorrect way. He might think it perfectly acceptable to go round in a pale green Terylene three-piece with six-inch wide lapels and a tie with a knot the size of a cottage loaf, looking like an out-of-work hairdresser, but I happened to believe in such old-fashioned traditions as good English cloth and decent English tailoring. Armitage laughed in a superior way and said that if success had anything to do with it, he'd rather be mistaken for an out-of-work hairdresser than the poor man's Anthony Eden any day. I replied that it was very easy to sneer at Anthony Eden, but that in my book, if we had a foreign secretary today who dressed half as well as he did, we might carry a little more weight at the international conference table. Armitage said, 'Churchill went round dressed in an old boiler suit, but he was still prime minister.' I simply could not be bothered to argue with him, and turned my attentions instead to the *Financial Times* Ordinary Share Index. I only wish someone could explain what it all means. I also wish I could find a single reference to Benganese Conglomerates.

## Tuesday, February 21st

Foolishly happened to mention to Beddoes that I had invested a monkey on a snip. He looked completely baffled and said he hadn't the faintest idea what I was talking about. I said, 'I thought as a City man you were familiar with the jargon. I was saying that I had invested five hundred pounds on a sure-fire winner.' He said that he had been in the City for twelve years but he had never heard any of those expressions used by anyone. 'If you really *do* work in the City,' I said quietly.

He said, 'What is this so-called snip that you have invested your monkey in, then?'

I said, 'Benganese Conglomerates.'

'Benganese Conglomerates?' he exclaimed.

I smiled and nodded.

Beddoes said, 'I wouldn't touch those with a barge pole. They're a real flash in the pan. Australian Mining all over again.' I was completely taken aback and reminded him that he had told me he was not on that side of the business.

'I'm not,' he said, 'but anyone with the slightest knowledge will tell you that Benganese Conglomerates are a bummer.'

I said, 'I think I will allow my stockbroker to be the best judge of that.' And left the room closing the door firmly behind me.

## Wednesday, February 22nd

Rang Tim first thing and said that a little dicky bird had just whispered in my ear that Benganese Conglomerates were a dead loss. He said, 'I don't know what sort of dicky birds you mix with, but this one is pulling your worm.' And he gave a not very convincing laugh.

I do not pretend to have a lot in common with Onassis, but I fancy I have a pretty good nose when it comes to sharp practice. I said, 'That may be so or it may not. At all events, I should like you to sell my shares immediately.'

'Don't be a bloody fool,' he said. 'If you sell now, you'll lose a penny per share; but if you are patient, you could make yourself a small fortune.' The only good decisions in business are the ones that are made quickly, and I wasted no time over this one.

'Sell,' I told him, and hung up. I do not know whether Sarah was listening in or not, but I have the feeling her attitude towards me has suddenly become unusually respectful.

## Thursday, February 23rd

No copies of the *FT* at the station this morning. I can't say I was entirely sorry. The *Daily Mirror* made an excellent substitute. Turned to page three to find a photograph of a girl with magnificent breasts who looked exactly like Beddoes's ex-girlfriend Jackie. According to the caption her name is Annabelle de Woolf, but that does not mean anything these days. It wouldn't surprise me a bit if she hadn't acted in a blue movie or two before now. Read a long and fascinating article about soccer hooliganism. Curiously enough, I have never once attended a first-class soccer match. Perhaps I should. It might be very useful to see some of this violence at close quarters.

## Friday, February 24th

Tackled Armitage re this question of a football match. He suggests tomorrow's game at Chelsea, and says there is sure to be some rough stuff. This is excellent news. Tim rang after lunch in a great state to ask if I'd seen the evening papers. Apparently Benganese Conglomerates have taken off even more dramatically than he had forecast. He has made a small personal fortune, and is already talking about changing his BMW for a Ferrari. I said I hoped he had not taken my instructions too literally the other afternoon.

'Of course I did,' he said. 'I'm a stockbroker, not a mind reader, more's the pity. Still, you only lost twenty pounds. On the other hand you could have made yourself four hundred; but that's the stock market for you.'

Beddoes was looking a damned sight too cheerful for my liking when he came in this evening. I was in no mood for pussyfooting, and told him straight out that he owed me £420. Of course he feigned total innocence, and when I explained why, he said, 'It's no good your taking my word on these things. I've told you already, I don't work on that side of the business.'

I said the only satisfaction to be derived from the whole sorry affair was that he had not gone into Benganese Conglomerates himself.

'Oh,' he said, 'I did. Made myself a tidy packet, as a matter of fact.' I told him that I was now quite convinced that he was a man who was totally incapable of telling the difference between right and wrong.

'The difference is crystal clear to me,' he said. 'I got it right, and you got it wrong.'

## Saturday, February 25th

Set off for the match in my oldest clothes and thickest shoes, having first made sure I had some 10p pieces in my pocket which in case of trouble I could quickly slip between my fingers and make into a knuckleduster. Arrived rather later than I had hoped, as a result of having to make a few small adjustments to the headlights on my scooter. Decided to park a good, safe distance from the ground, and joined the fans in their blue-and-white scarves. They certainly looked a pretty rough crowd to me, and I was glad of my coins. After much jostling and horseplay at one of the side entrances, I was confronted by a hefty-looking man with an official badge on his arm who told me, 'Sorry, no entrance without a ticket.' It had not occurred to me before that one had to book in advance, and I was on the point of making an official complaint when I felt a hand on my shoulder. Spun round to find myself face to face with Hugh Bryant-Fenn, of all people, who said he had a spare ticket if it would interest me. In spite of our lateness, we managed to find a couple of seats with an excellent view of the whole pitch, and settled down to enjoy the game. I pulled my coat collar up high around my neck so that, in the event of receiving a bottle on the back of the head, I could be sure of some protection. However, the first half passed off without incident, and not one of the fans around us showed the slightest sign of wishing to pick a fight with me or anyone else.

'Not much hooliganism today then,' I murmured to Hugh out of the corner of my mouth. He looked surprised.

'I wouldn't know about that,' he said. 'That sort of thing happens down on the terraces, not here in the numbered seats.'

Chelsea won 3–1, not that it mattered a hoot to me one way or the other. An unfortunate incident occurred after the game when I became involved in a misunderstanding with a passing motorist outside the ground. Heated words were being exchanged when a policeman appeared from nowhere and told me to turn out my pockets.

Naturally, I protested in the strongest possible terms, explaining that if it was anyone's fault it was the driver's for not looking where he was going. I might have been addressing a lump of wood for all the sympathy I received, and it was with extreme reluctance that I acceded to his request. I had quite forgotten that I was still carrying the spanner, and the policeman pounced upon it with a cry of satisfaction. 'Hullo,' he said. 'Looking for a bit of aggro, were you?' I told him that I had never been so insulted.

'If you think that's an insult,' he said, 'wait till you get down to the station.' And before I knew what, I was frog-marched away, bundled into a police van along with half a dozen vicious-looking youths and driven off at high speed to Chelsea police station. One of them, who had a safety pin through his nose and a length of lavatory chain hanging from his ear lobe, said: 'What you been up to then, dad? Misbehaving with small boys?'

Fortunately, there was a policeman present, and I pretended not to have heard. Upon arrival at the police station, I informed the desk sergeant that I wished to speak to my solicitor but was told to wait my turn with the rest.

It was not until my name was called out and I was asked for my solicitor's name that I realized that I did not actually have one. Luckily, I was able to remember the name of father's solicitor in Kent. His wife answered the phone and said she was very sorry but her husband had died on Tuesday and she was just leaving for the funeral.

I remember seeing a film on TV about a man who is wrongly arrested and accused of murder, but is unable to persuade anyone of his innocence, and that is precisely how I felt as the sergeant took down my statement. It soon became obvious, of course, that it was all a misunderstanding and after a cup of tea I was told I could go home.

I am seriously considering bringing a complaint against the police for false arrest. But first I must find myself a solicitor.

## Tuesday, February 28th

I have just about had enough of Beddoes's constant reference to prisons and criminals. This evening he introduced me to this new girlfriend of his, Birgit, as 'the well-known jailbird'. I was strongly tempted to point out that, if throwing away a tub of mustard and cress that does not belong to you is not a criminal act, I'd like to know what is, but could not be bothered to waste my breath. How a man who contributes to the sale of pornographic material can seriously sit there puffing away at one of his ill-gotten cigars and accuse anyone else of disreputable behaviour is beyond me. Talk about mote and beam.

# March

### Thursday, March 2nd

I am reminded of Hugh Bryant-Fenn's joke that if the actress Tuesday Weld had married Frederick March II, she would have become Tuesday March II. It always makes me chuckle. But of course it doesn't really apply this year.

### Friday, March 3rd

Suddenly realized that I have now had my wildlife book for over ten days, so shall not be able to send it back as I had hoped. This is probably just as well, since the postage on a book of that size is almost as much as the book itself. Besides, it's always useful to have in the car. One never knows when one might need to find one's way to Whipsnade Zoo, or identify a bird one has just run over. I am also sure that the people who keep the book stand a better chance of winning the Wildlife Game than the ones who send them back.

### Saturday, March 4th

Jane has gone to Oxted for the weekend, thank goodness. Our affair is not going at all well, and I have grave doubts about our future together. Matters are not improved by her insistence on wearing her National Health frames despite the fact that her other pair have been ready for collection for several days now. I am sure she does it purely to reproach me. Her increasing plainness might be less obvious if it were not for Birgit's great beauty. I simply do not understand what she sees in Beddoes. I suppose it's all to do with sex, as usual.

## Sunday, March 5th

Had a most erotic dream about Birgit last night. She was dressed in a policeman's uniform and wearing a pair of National Health glasses which made her look more desirable than ever.

I hope I am not falling in love with Birgit. It could complicate matters no end.

## Monday, March 6th

Armitage marched into my office this morning and said in an off-hand way, 'If you're not doing anything better on Saturday, we're having a few friends round for a bit of a do. We'd love to see you. Alone preferably.'

I suppose by 'we' he must mean himself and Sarah. At all events, it is not *my* way of inviting someone to a party. However, am quite looking forward to it already. Knowing Armitage he is sure to have laid on a few pretty girls with loose morals, and after all, it's not as though I were married to Jane.

## Tuesday, March 7th

Flirted outrageously with a most attractive dark-haired girl on the Tube this morning. Am only sorry I did not have time to follow it up. She was obviously pretty easy meat, and I noticed that the moment I got out she went straight across and sat next to a chap who had been standing next to me all the way from Notting Hill Gate. What *is* coming over me these days?

## Thursday, March 9th

This evening, I kissed Birgit on the cheek while Beddoes was in the lavatory. Heaven knows what made me do it. All I know is that it seemed the most natural thing in the world. Instead of being shocked or angry, as I had expected, she merely smiled and went on watching TV. There is definitely electricity there between us, and as long as things like this can happen, it would be quite wrong of me to consider tying myself down to one woman.

### Friday, March 10th

Nothing of interest to report. To bed early, which was probably just as well the way I'm going.

### Saturday, March 11th

To Armitage's party.

I have long suspected that he moves with a fast crowd for whom drug-taking and other forms of loose behaviour are very much second nature, and it seems I was not mistaken. A strange aroma hung over the proceedings, and although I have never partaken myself, only a fool would have failed to recognize it for what it was.

Got into conversation with a girl with an appallingly scarred face who offered me a cigarette from what looked like an innocent packet of Players No. 6, but I was not taking any chances, and left her to puff away contentedly. It is always difficult to know what to say to someone who has obviously suffered a serious misfortune. Some people try and ignore it, but I have always believed you should bring it out into the open quite naturally. I said, 'I'm so sorry about your face. How did it happen?'

She replied calmly, 'In the normal way. I just mixed up the henna, took out a small brush and painted it on.' I managed to laugh off my *faux pas* but could not help reflecting that, as make-up goes, hers was in a particularly bad taste.

Later a huge risotto was brought in. Sarah came up and told me she had found the recipe in her Alice B. Toklas cook book, the implication obviously being that one or two ingredients had been added of a somewhat spicier nature than usual. I know pot is supposed to be non-addictive and less harmful than a whisky and soda, but there are exceptions to every rule, and although I do not see myself trying to fly off the mantelpiece, I was not about to make a fool of myself in front of anyone – let alone people from the office. Apart from allowing myself one small mouthful from the henna-ed girl's plate, I stuck firmly to wine. Even so, I began to feel quite light-headed and had the strangest feeling that everything in the room was advancing and receding from me in an oddly surrealistic way. By the end of the evening I was in such a peculiar state that Roundtree had to drive me home and put me to bed. All very embarrassing, but a lesson well worth learning.

## Sunday, March 12th

One often hears it said that one of the great things about pot is that it does not give you a hangover. I do not know what it was they put in the risotto last night, but I would rather have gone the whole hog and tried to fly out of the window than have had to suffer what I have suffered today. I am too ill to write any more.

## Monday, March 13th

To work rather later than usual, still feeling decidedly shaky. Surprised to find Sarah as bright and perky as ever, apparently having experienced no ill-effects at all. Same thing with Armitage, who bounced into my office at eleven-thirty, noisy and extremely full of himself.

'My word,' he said, 'you were certainly knocking back the wine the other night. You really should have had some of that risotto. It's always a great mistake to drink heavily on an empty stomach.' I suppose that in his circle you have to keep up pretences for the sake of the outside world.

## Tuesday, March 14th

Feeling marginally better this morning. Was in the middle of a not very important Barford meeting in Roundtree's office when Sarah rang through to say she had some television people on the line asking for me urgently. My first thought was that it was 'This is Your Life' people at last, but to my surprise I found myself speaking to Nicola Benson. I have not seen her since we used to appear in undergraduate revues at Oxford. It seems that she is now something very high up in television. She is busy planning a major new series for BBC 2 and thinks that I might be just the person to anchor it. I do not quite understand what this would entail, but it all sounds most exciting, and I am to lunch with her and her executive producer on Friday to talk about it further. One often hears of people suddenly being plucked out of obscurity to become TV stars, but somehow one never thinks of it happening to oneself. Why not, though?

## Thursday, March 16th

Am so excited at the prospect of tomorrow's lunch that nothing else seems worth mentioning.

## Friday, March 17th

Lunched with Nicola at the Terrazza, always a great favourite of mine, but scarcely noticed what we ate or drank. All I did notice was how very much more attractive she was than I had remembered. At Oxford I could hardly be bothered to give her the time of day, yet now I feel she is a girl I could go for in a very big way indeed. What a strange thing life is. Her executive producer, a cocky young man called John, explained the idea of the programme which is to take a typical young man about town and transport him to a remote part of northern Scotland with a minimum supply of modern aids, and see how well he succeeds in looking after himself – building a hut, hunting for food, etc.

It is a far cry from sitting in a studio chatting to interesting people which was how I had envisaged the programme, and I must confess that at first I was disappointed. On the other hand, as I pointed out, it was an extraordinary coincidence that they should have picked on self-sufficiency, a subject which I had only recently researched at close quarters. They agreed that it was rather extraordinary, and that they had obviously been quite right to think of me. However, they warned that before any firm decision could be arrived at, I should have to undergo some sort of test to find out how I reacted to a camera and so on. I pointed out that I was a very busy man and might not necessarily be free at the drop of a hat. John said he thought it would probably be some time next week, but that he would be in touch nearer the time.

As we were leaving the restaurant, Nicola said, 'I know that a self-sufficiency programme on BBC 2 may not seem at first glance very glamorous, but if this thing catches on – and we think it will – it could turn you into a very big television star.'

Spent the afternoon practising my autograph and went home early. The temptation to break the news to the others in the flat was almost unbearable, but am determined to say nothing until I know for certain. I have no wish to make a fool of myself.

## Saturday, March 18th

For the first time in weeks, found myself alone in the flat this evening with Jane.

I have definitely come to the conclusion that I could do a great deal better for myself – and if all goes well, probably shall. Even so, I am pretty fed up with her bossy attitude towards everything I say or do. This evening, for example, she said, 'Do you know, you're becoming a real telly bug. You have watched everything from "Dr Who" onwards.'

I explained that I had to do it for professional reasons, and that it was not exactly something I enjoyed. Any normal girl would have asked me what I meant. However, there's no doubt she is intrigued.

## Monday, March 20th

Nothing from the television people, but I suppose it is early days yet. Snubbed Armitage in a Marketing Strategy meeting.

## Tuesday, March 21st

Took Jane to dinner at the Bordelino and broke the news to her over coffee. Although she appeared indifferent, I'm pretty sure that deep down she is beginning to regret not taking her chances when she had them. To underline the point, I said, 'It's extraordinary to think that tonight I am able to walk into this restaurant, just like that, and no one gives me a second look; nobody knows who I am and nobody cares. And yet in a few weeks from now I'll walk into this same restaurant and people will stop talking, and point, and whisper, and the waiters will scurry about and make a lot of fuss of me and ask me to sign the menu, and I'll be obliged to leave a larger tip than usual with the woman who looks after the coats. And yet basically I'll be exactly the same person.'

She thought for a moment and said, 'I simply could not bear to go out with someone famous. It would be too embarrassing for words.' That's what she *says*.

## Wednesday, March 22nd

Thinking back to last night, I am beginning to understand now how Plantagenet Palliser must have felt when faced with the decision of giving up the chancellorship of the exchequer or his marriage. How can a man, who is unable to order his own affairs, dare to attempt to direct those of the nation? Or for that matter of BBC television? I am seriously beginning to wonder if I should not consider giving the whole idea up.

## Thursday, March 23rd

Mystified not to have heard anything still from the television people. As a result have been quite unable to get down to any serious work.

Finally, after lunch, rang Nicola's office. The phone was answered by a secretary. I told her that I was Mr Crisp's assistant and that I was ringing to say that he had had to go away for a few days on urgent business but that if they had any news, I would be glad to pass it on. The girl said she knew nothing about it. She also asked who Mr Crisp was, which is ominous, to say the least.

## Friday, March 24th

Nicola rang at last to say that there had been a slight setback to their plans, but there was nothing to worry about and they would be calling me next week to fix a date for the test. It's just as well, since a small spot has suddenly come up on the side of my nose.

Victoria has suddenly become more friendly of late. Women are all the same: the tiniest sniff of fame and they all come running. I suppose it is something I shall have to come to terms with.

## Saturday, March 25th

To Kent for the Easter weekend – alone.

Finally succeeded in distracting mother's attention away from the cat sufficiently to give her my news. All she said was, 'That's nice, dear. Perhaps now you'll be asked on to "Any Questions" and meet Edward du Cann.'

Spent the whole of the afternoon trying to build a hut at the bottom of the garden with my bare hands. It is a good deal more difficult than it sounds, and the fact that mother's garden consists of quarter of an acre of lawn and two small flower beds tested my powers of survival to their limits. Mother could not have been less helpful if she had tried.

I tried to tell her that the programme was an experiment in living; but she replied that, as far as she was concerned, it was an experiment in being very silly indeed and that anyway tea was on the table and if I didn't come at once it would be stewed.

After tea, I constructed a makeshift tent out of a broom, a garden fork and the cat's blanket. Mother had to point out the obvious fact that the chances of my coming across a cat's blanket in the wilds of northern Scotland were remote in the extreme. I explained that, in the nature of things, it could only be a simulated model and that the object of this particular experiment was simply to see if I could survive a night out in the open in the middle of winter. She asked me what I was planning to do for food – make a surprise raid on Mrs Agar's bantams down the road, or slum it on worms and leatherjackets? And added that if I really thought she had nothing better to do than make up my bed and get in half a rolled shoulder of lamb specially, then I had another think coming.

I said that when the time came I would probably snare a rabbit or shoot a ptarmigan with a rough bow and arrow, and repeated that my concern for the present was sleeping and keeping warm.

Set off into the garden shortly after eleven, with a pile of straw and wood shavings from a box in the garage which had been used to deliver a special offer spin drier.

All was going to plan, and I was just settling down with the help of my old skiing anorak and an extra pair of thick

'She had also taken the opportunity of bringing two cellular blankets, a cushion, a hot-water bottle and a cup of Bovril.'

socks, when mother arrived to say that the cat wouldn't settle and would I mind changing the blanket for an old one she had found in a trunk in the spare room. She had also taken the opportunity of bringing two cellular blankets, a cushion, a hot-water bottle and a cup of Bovril.

Finally dozed off at about two-thirty.

Surprisingly warm.

## Sunday, March 26th

Easter Day.

Mother woke me with a cup of tea at seven. I do not believe I have slept so well or felt so fit for years. Suddenly, Easter has taken on a whole new meaning for me. Was so excited that, despite a badly thought-out sermon, I put two pounds in the collection plate at Mattins.

## Monday, March 27th

Returned to London to find a letter from the managing director of the company that put on the sex show. I had forgotten all about it. He says that he is amazed by my comments; the show is a great success and this is the first complaint he has received. And not the last, I shouldn't wonder, if many more people start having the sort of dreams I had. I notice he says nothing about returning my money. I am in two minds whether to refer the matter to a higher authority.

## Tuesday, March 28th

Rang Nicola about my night of survival, but she was in a meeting, so left a message to call me back. I do think it's important to be seen to be taking an *active* interest. None of us is so good at our job that we cannot do with a few helpful suggestions now and then.

## Wednesday, March 29th

Have suddenly gone quite mad and ordered a pair of contact lenses – the ordinary hard variety. I know some people think I look rather well in my glasses, and they certainly have not done any noticeable harm to Ludovic Kennedy's career.

Still, I cannot help feeling that, in matters of communication, glasses do tend to act as a sort of psychological barrier, and actually I happen to think I look marginally better without them.

The man who tried them on for me in the shop had such bad breath that I felt quite sick. Most relieved when he suggested I should walk around the streets for twenty minutes or so and see how I got on. In fact unable to see anything or to get on much either due to the tears that poured continually from my eyes. It is just like a severe attack of hay fever. I have never actually suffered from hay fever but imagine that is what it is like. Was so blinded at one point that I went hard into a lamp post, bruising my forehead painfully and dislodging one of the lenses. Decided to return at once to the shop, but by now rendered virtually sightless and had to be shown the way by Irish traffic warden. It took over five minutes to remove the lenses, during which time the optician breathed malodorously into my face.

I have agreed to go ahead with a pair, and only hope that I shall not suffer a Pavlovian reaction and feel violently ill every time I take them out or put them in.

## Thursday, March 30th

A message from Nicola's office to say that they should have a definite answer for me next week. If they mean a definite *date*, why don't they say so? For people whose job is communication they seem to have a curiously slap-happy way of using the language.

## Friday, March 31st

Rang the local telephone manager's office and asked for my number to be made ex-directory. One of the many drawbacks of being a public figure is that one lays oneself wide open to unsolicited phone calls.

Last year Mollie Marsh-Gibbon was rung up every day regularly for a week by a man who said, 'Next time we meet it's roll-ons and panties down and smacked bottoms for you.'

Not that Mollie is a public figure – and as a matter of fact I think she secretly enjoyed it – but as the man in the telephone manager's office agreed, you can never be too sure these days. It was perfectly normal for TV people to go ex-directory and by an odd coincidence the new A–D books were due to go to press any day now, and he would look into it straight away. I doubt if I would have received such prompt service if I had been just any old member of the public.

# April

### Saturday, April 1st

Woke this morning to find a note pushed under the door. It was from Beddoes to say that someone had rung while I was out last night to know if I would be interested in taking over from Michael Parkinson, and, if so, would I ring the controller of BBC 1 as soon as possible.

Had just dialled the number when I heard shrieks of laughter from the next room and Beddoes and Jane came in shouting, 'Who's an April fool, then?'

They all roared till the tears ran.

I'm afraid I was unable to see the funny side of it. A stupid joke like that could destroy a man's career in seconds.

### Sunday, April 2nd

An uneventful, unproductive day, filled with doubts and misgivings.

### Monday, April 3rd

Am in a quandary to know what to wear for the television test. The pin-stripe is probably rather too formal. I do not wish to appear stuffy. Nor do I think that the brown tweed suit strikes quite the thrusting note that I am sure they are looking for. Finally decide on an excellent compromise. A velvet suit. Dark brown, perhaps, or bottle green. Elegant and slightly daring with a touch of cosiness.

Set off at lunchtime for the shops. Walking along Oxford Street I had the distinct feeling that people were looking at me in a quite different way from usual. But, of course, it is quite well known that fame – or even imminent fame – can imbue hitherto quite ordinary people with a peculiar aura which sets them apart from the crowd. I remember I once saw Stewart Granger outside Safeways wearing a safari outfit. Somehow one simply could not help looking at him. It is most interesting to notice how quickly and effortlessly I am beginning to acquire some of that star quality myself. Very pleased with the suit. It is dark blue. Victoria said that she has never been able to resist men in velvet. She seems to have very little difficulty with me.

## Wednesday, April 5th

Horrified to realize, while shaving this morning, just how pale I am looking. This evening borrowed Victoria's sun lamp and had a session while listening to an indifferent radio programme. A light tan can do me nothing but good, although, of course, people with black and white sets will hardly reap the benefit. The effect so far is rather on the red side, but I daresay if I keep it up for a few days, it will gradually turn brown. The white rings round the eyes are a bit of a worry, too.

## Thursday, April 6th

Was on my way out to an early lunch when the phone rang. It was John, the executive producer, to say that there had been a muddle over budgets and that they had had to re-think the programme in terms of a studio discussion. This could not have suited me better, and I told him so. He said, 'Well, actually that rather puts you out of court, I'm afraid. Frankly, you just haven't got the weight to carry that sort of thing.'

I am not up in this media jargon and asked him what sort of person he had in mind.

'We're thinking in terms of Michael Parkinson,' he said.

I do not understand any of it, and neither, I suspect, do they. All I do know is that I am landed with a blue velvet suit and a pair of contact lenses which I now no longer need nor want.

### Friday, April 7th

Took the suit back at lunchtime. They were not at all pleased. Neither was I when they gave me a credit note for £39·50. When I told the manager I would prefer the cash, he said, 'I daresay you would, sir.'

I tried on a three-piece in a Prince of Wales check, but found I looked exactly like Armitage. Couldn't get out of it fast enough. Nothing else caught my eye. I might just as well have kept the blue velvet after all.

Suddenly life seems extraordinarily flat.

### Saturday, April 8th

Unless I am much mistaken, something very fishy is going on between Beddoes and Jane. When I walked into the sitting room this evening, I had the distinct feeling that they had been kissing each other. Beddoes said, 'Oh, hello, matey. I've just been trying to get a fly out of Jane's eye.' But no amount of levity could conceal the obvious guilt on both their faces.

If she thinks that by throwing herself at another man's head she is going to make me come running, I am afraid she is much mistaken.

### Sunday, April 9th

Unable to sleep a wink last night for thinking about Beddoes and Jane. It is not jealousy that consumes me, but indignation at Beddoes's attitude that anyone is fair game. The one chance in the week to get a really good night's sleep completely ruined.

Was reading the papers after lunch when Beddoes breezed in and announced that he and Jane were just off to the cinema and would I like to join them. I replied pointedly that I was not in the habit of playing gooseberry, and besides I did not hold with cinema-going on Sundays.

He said, 'Please yourself,' and left – for some cheap hotel in Paddington, I shouldn't wonder. Happily I am beyond caring.

Victoria continues to be friendly, if reserved. She says that she has seen Mike again, but that he is very mixed up and depressed about his failed marriage, and does not think there is any future for them. I know it's wrong, but I must admit I am immensely cheered by the news. It would just serve Jane right if I did catch Victoria on the rebound. I have decided, for the time being at any rate, to say nothing about the failure of the TV programme.

## Monday, April 10th

Armitage said, 'You *might* catch her on the rebound, but if I were you, I'd stand well back.'

That is absolutely the last time I ever confide in him. Dave Garwood rang to say he had been trying to get hold of me all weekend over a matter of some freelance work, but had been unable to find my number. He had lost his A–D directory and when he rang Directory Enquiries, they had told him that they were not at liberty to give him my number since it was now listed as ex-directory.

I had completely forgotten about this and rang the telephone manager to ask if my name could be reinstated in the book after all, but he said I was too late since they had already gone to press. This effectively puts paid to anyone I do not know ringing me up with offers of work.

One small crumb of consolation: I have a feeling I may be able to get the contact lenses off tax.

## Tuesday, April 11th

I have never been so bored at work. Armitage tried to score off me in a meeting this morning, but I simply could not have cared less.

## Wednesday, April 12th

Watched an old Cary Grant film this evening. I have always rather identified with him. Interested to notice that he is actually much broader across the beam than I had realized. I do not know why I should find this so cheering, but I do.

## Thursday, April 13th

The most terrible thing happened today. I was in a meeting in Prout's office discussing the Merchandising Development

Programme for the new Barford project when I gave such an enormous yawn that my jaws became locked wide open. I struggled for half an hour to close them but in the end had to take a taxi to the Middlesex Hospital where they gave me a local anaesthetic and did the job for me. It would not have been so bad if I had not had to wait for over an hour in a crowded out-patients' department.

A small boy who was sitting opposite could not take his eyes off me. Finally his mother said to him, 'You shouldn't stare like that. He can't help being wrong in the head.'

Naturally I attempted to register my complaint but all that came out was an unpleasant gargling sound. At this the woman seized the child by the arm and bundled him away to the other end of the room.

Without question the most humiliating day of my life.

## Friday, April 14th

I daresay there are people who would accuse me of turning Victoria's unhappiness to my own advantage. I do not see it that way at all. I obviously represent for her a safe harbour after storm-tossed seas. After all, what are friends for if they cannot proffer comfort in times of need? If she doesn't need it, she is perfectly at liberty to say so.

## Saturday, April 15th

A sensational turn of events. Mike Pritchard rang to say that he had woken this morning to discover that during the night all his hair had fallen out. He had found it lying beside him on the pillow like a small sleeping cat. He sounded pretty shaken. Victoria announced that, of course, she would have to go to him at once. I don't really see why. He has lost so much hair already, I wouldn't have thought that losing the lot would make very much difference one way or the other. Still, who am I to dissuade her?

All I can do now is wait and see how she feels when she returns. Waited up till one, but still no sign of her, so went to bed, a deeply disillusioned man.

## Sunday, April 16th

Woke early after a troubled night to find a strange smell in the flat. Discovered that amid all the excitement last night, I had forgotten to take the bœuf bourguignon out of the oven, as a result of which it had become welded onto the casserole. Threw the whole thing into the dustbin. No sign of Victoria all morning.

Beddoes appeared bleary-eyed at lunchtime, followed shortly by a large angry Italian lady whom he introduced as Stephania. She completely took over the kitchen, regardless of the fact that I was trying to cook myself lunch, and proceeded to make herself and Beddoes an enormous cheese omelette. She was not only extremely messy but also very noisy, and kept shouting out to Beddoes at the top of her voice through the kitchen door. I felt compelled to point out that we had recently suffered a tragedy in the household and I would be obliged if she would respect other people's feelings. Naturally she got hold of the wrong end of the stick and started jabbering away at me in Italian and rolling her eyes, and would, I have no doubt, have assaulted me physically had Beddoes not appeared in the doorway and let out an enormous bellow. He certainly knows how to keep his women under control, I'll give him that.

Where Jane is, I have no idea. Or Victoria, come to that. It's like living in a madhouse.

## Monday, April 17th

Jane walked into the flat this evening after work, glared at me, and without a word, stormed into her bedroom and slammed the door behind her. I mentioned this extraordinary behaviour to Beddoes when he came in. He said, 'I'm not surprised, the way you've treated her in the last few days.'

I was perfectly astounded and said that if anyone had treated her poorly it was him -- making great play for her one minute, then throwing her over in favour of some mad Italian woman the next. Beddoes said, 'Why should I make any play for her, great or small? She's *your* friend. Besides, she's not nearly pretty enough for my liking.'

He must take me for a complete fool.

I wondered if I should talk the whole thing over with Jane, but decided to let sleeping dogs lie. Now that I have finally made the break and things are going well with Victoria, there's no point in raking over old coals. As Beddoes once remarked, you've got to be cruel to be kind in these matters – except, of course, that in his case, he's cruel to be cruel.

Still no sign of Victoria. I am beginning to fear the worst.

### Tuesday, April 18th

Victoria rang at last to say that Mike needed her and she had decided to return to him after all, and would I be very kind and run a few of her things over in the car – including her blue woolly hat. I suppose I should have kicked up a fuss. But really what is the point?

### Thursday, April 20th

Victoria came round to collect a few remaining bits and pieces and to say goodbye. I do not mind admitting that tears came to my eyes as she kissed me on the cheek. I only hope she knows what she's doing.

Lying in bed this evening, I decided that it really does not pay to saddle oneself with lame ducks, and I do not intend to do so again. In fact, I have no intention of saddling myself with anyone. Beddoes has got the right idea. Play fast and loose; it's the only way.

The London Season is about to burst upon us at any moment and, taking that as a basis, I shall throw myself wholeheartedly into society and live purely for pleasure from now on. Marriage can wait – probably for ever. It brings nothing but unhappiness.

### Friday, April 21st

To the opticians to collect my contact lenses. Enormously cheered to find a different fitter in attendance. His breath could not have been fresher. Unfortunately, just as he leaned forward to place the first lens in my eye, I noticed he had something nasty protruding from his left nostril. I do not know which made me feel iller: that or the thought of the quite unnecessary expense.

## Saturday, April 22nd

Read a most fascinating article in the paper this morning about Venice. According to its author, unless drastic steps are taken to stop the industrial pollution that is eating away the façades and the very foundations of this beautiful city – and taken very soon – Venice, as we know it, will cease to exist. Ashamed to realize that I do not actually know it at all, and so have decided to get out there as soon as possible to find out for myself what all the fuss is about.

## Sunday, April 23rd

St George's Day and the birthday of our greatest poet and dramatist. To be perfectly honest, I have always found Shakespeare's plays rather difficult to follow and wonder if too much isn't made of him altogether.

## Monday, April 24th

Rang Hugh Bryant-Fenn re Venice. He is always going over there in his capacity as chairman of the British Carpaccio Society, and has written one or two good articles about the place.

By an odd coincidence he is planning to go himself next week and suggests that I should join him. He says he should be able to get any number of 'freebies', as he calls them, at all the best hotels.

I asked him which of us should get the tickets. 'Oh,' he said, 'I think you had better make your own travel arrangements. I shall probably go as the guest of some airline or other.'

I asked him, half-jokingly, if he couldn't take me along free as his assistant. He told me that would be quite out of the question, but that he'd see I was all right once we got there. I presume this means he will be organizing a 'freebie' for me in one of the hotels he was talking about, but didn't like to ask outright.

## Tuesday, April 25th

To my local travel agent to buy my ticket for Venice. The Getaway Weekend comprising return flight, bed and breakfast for three nights in a first-class hotel and free transfers to and from the airport certainly sounds excellent value, but not, of course, if one is being given one's accommodation free anyway, and I settled for just the return air fare.

This evening Jane said if I wasn't doing anything at the weekend, perhaps I might like to go down to Oxted with her. I explained about Venice. She was not quite as impressed as I had hoped.

## Wednesday, April 26th

To Hatchards to look for a good guide book on Venice. The *Companion Guide* seems as good value as any. Bumped into Mollie Marsh-Gibbon who announced that Venice was the most overrated tourist trap in Europe.

There appear to be as many opinions about this subject as there are people who give them. Thank goodness I shall soon be in a position to speak upon the matter with some authority.

## Friday, April 28th

Woken at the crack of dawn by Bryant-Fenn to say he would not now be able to get away until tomorrow morning, but that if I went to the Hotel Browning and asked for Signor Domenico and mentioned his name, I would be well looked after. We have arranged to meet tomorrow morning at eleven on the Rialto Bridge.

On the plane sat next to a man whose face seemed very familiar, but for the life of me I could not put a name to it. I am normally very good at remembering names. Eventually we got talking, but although I asked him all manner of questions, he left me none the wiser. Finally, I steered the conversation round to the subject of passports and how unrecognizable people were in their photographs. I said, 'I mean, just look at this dreadful picture of me,' and handed my passport to him. Naturally I assumed he would reciprocate with his, but all he did was look at mine, roar with laughter and hand it back again. Soon after that he went to sleep. The flight seemed never-ending; nor was it made any the shorter by the couple sitting behind me. There was apparently nothing he did not know about Italy, Italian art and Venice. If only she had known *something*, she might have been able to staunch the flow of information that poured from him ceaselessly. At one stage he struck up a conversation in loud, obviously schoolboy Italian, with an Italian family sitting opposite. As we were disembarking, I turned to him and remarked in a loud voice that he was obviously quite an expert on Italy.

'I should be,' he replied, 'I am an Italian and I am bringing my new English bride home to visit my family here in Venice.' He went on to explain that he was a lecturer in Italian art at some college in London, and added that if there was anything he could do for me during my stay, he would be only too delighted. He knew one of the leading hoteliers intimately and would be very happy to show me some of the work that's being carried out on the famous bronze horses on the front of St Mark's. I thanked him and said that I was already being well looked after.

Finally arrived at the Hotel Browning. It had a warm, welcoming look to it, although it was far from de luxe. Asked for Signor Domenico only to be informed that the hotel had recently changed hands and he had gone to Pisa. Mentioned Hugh's name but it meant nothing to the receptionist. However, have decided to stay anyway. It is a little further from the centre than I should have liked, but it is not all that expensive and anyway tomorrow I shall be moving into something a good deal more comfortable with Hugh. It hardly seemed worth unpacking, but I did remove a few valuable items from my case, such as travellers' cheques, passport, wallet, guide book etc., and concealed them beneath the spare blanket in the wardrobe.

Interested to note that the decay is already beginning to work its way indoors. It is particularly noticeable just behind my bed.

## Saturday, April 29th

Woken early by sun streaming through tear in curtains. Threw open windows and breathed in morning air. Apart from nasty smell from small canal below, a perfect morning. After breakfast, checked out of hotel, and made my way plus suitcase to Grand Canal where I caught a *vaporetto* to St Mark's Square. No sooner entered St Mark's than I remembered I had left my guide book, cheques, passport, etc.,

'*He finally rolled up at ten to one, if you please, dressed in
blue sleeveless shirt, shorts and sandals.*'

under spare blanket in hotel wardrobe. No time to go all the way back, so rang the manager to ask them to look after it until later. As a result had to cut down visit to Cathedral and Doge's Palace to twenty minutes.

Even so, arrived at Rialto Bridge twenty minutes late. No sign of Hugh. He finally rolled up at ten to one, if you please, dressed in blue sleeveless shirt, shorts and sandals. I don't know why, but sandals always set my teeth on edge, especially when worn with socks. I might have expected Hugh to dress like that abroad, but that did not make them any the more bearable. He offered no explanation or apology for his lateness, but merely announced that it was time for lunch. I asked him where he was planning to take me. He replied that he disliked making plans when travelling and preferred to walk about until he found somewhere that took his fancy. I said that surely, as an old Venice hand, he must know of many good trattorias.

'Not in this part of town,' he snapped.

I suggested that in that case we might just as well go straight to his hotel where I could leave my suitcase and have lunch at the same time.

'Oh,' he said, 'are you turning out of the Browning then?'

I replied that I certainly was and explained why. He appeared quite unconcerned at being so utterly discredited and asked where I was planning to go. I said that, if I had understood him correctly, I would be moving in with him on a complementary basis. He replied that he had had enough trouble fixing himself up without worrying about me as well. I reminded him of all the 'freebies' we had heard so much about. He said, 'If there's one thing I can't stand, it's people who are not prepared to pay for their pleasures.'

Finally ate lunch in a funny little restaurant in a garden. Food excellent, if rather dear. When the bill arrived, Hugh said he couldn't bear fiddling about trying to divide bills into two, so why didn't I deal with this one and he'd pay for dinner.

'I know of a marvellous little place called the Madonna,' he said. 'All the Venetians eat there. The tourists haven't discovered it yet.'

On the way out, bumped into the art historian from the plane and his wife. I told him I'd very much like to take up his offer re the horses. He said he would call me at the hotel as soon as he knew what his plans were.

Afterwards Hugh told me his name was Carlo Mendotti and that he was one of the leading experts on Venetian art. Obviously we are very lucky to be asked, but Hugh said, 'I thought he sounded pretty keen to get out of it, if you ask me.' There is nothing I dislike more than professional jealousy.

Suggested popping in to the Accademia for a quick look at the Tintorettos and Canalettos. Hugh said that the only thing worth seeing there were the Carpaccios, and that anyway the best Carpaccios were in the church of San Giorgio del Schiavoni. 'You can see the Accademia any time,' he added.

I reminded him we had still made no arrangements re my accommodation. He replied, 'If I were you, I'd try and get your room back at the Browning tonight. I should have fixed up a freebie by tomorrow morning.'

Returned to Browning. My room already let, but luckily they were able to give me another, slightly cheaper, and actually I have always rather enjoyed sleeping in attics.

Left suitcase and set off for San Giorgio, but arrived just as they were closing for the night. Returned to Browning via Accademia which was also closed.

Was in the bath when Hugh rang to say he had been asked to dine with some marquesa and we should have to scrap our plans for dinner. In fact rather relieved. In my experience one always finds out so much more about a city on one's own.

Decided to try Madonna anyway. Arrived to find place jammed to the doors with groups of tourists and not a table to be had. In the end, ate a plate of risotto in a modest trattoria, felt rather ill and went to bed early.

My new room may be a little less spacious than last night's but the bed is certainly softer. Unfortunately, kept awake for rather a long time by couple in the next room making love – or possibly playing Italian Scrabble.

## Sunday, April 30th

Woken early by gondoliers shouting beneath my window. Another glorious sunny day.

Took the boat out to the island of Torcello for lunch at the famous Locanda Cipriani. Hugh assured me he would be able to change a travellers' cheque there, and that lunch was on him.

Arrived at restaurant in good time. A large room with tables spilling out into the garden. Ours was not exactly in the best position, but certainly not in the worst, and we had a good, if slightly restricted, view of the bottom half of the cathedral campanile.

Had just started on plate of green tagliatelle when Hugh said, 'Hullo,' and Carlo Mendotti and wife walked in and sat at a table near the garden. Finally caught their eye and nodded my head in the continental manner, but obviously they had not seen me after all. But then who sees anyone when one is in love?

Afterwards went across and spoke to them. Hugh said he knew when he was not wanted and disappeared mumbling something about the bill. Carlo full of fascinating information. He said he could remember a time when Torcello was a place for getting away from the tourists, but that these days it was worse than St Mark's Square. I said I quite agreed and that I expected I'd be seeing them again soon. Carlo said, 'Venice is very small. It is difficult to avoid people.'

Disappointed that he made no reference to our visit to the horses. Also that the restaurant refused to change Bryant-Fenn's travellers' cheques. I do not mind coughing up for everything on a temporary basis, but the fact is I am rapidly running out of cash myself. After a hurried visit to the cathedral to look at the mosaics, caught the boat back to Venice, with a view to seeing the Carpaccios in San Giorgio. Disembarked and went straight to nearest café for coffee and ice cream. Suddenly Carlo and his wife appeared from nowhere and sat down at a nearby table. Hugh muttered, 'This is getting downright embarrassing,' and leaping to his feet he marched off down the street.

There was nothing to do but pay the bill and set off after him. Luckily, I don't think the Mendottis saw me. Had words with Hugh, as a result of which we both completely lost our sense of direction and arrived at San Giorgio five minutes after closing time.

Agreed to meet Hugh for dinner at the Colomba at eight-thirty and returned to Browning. Arrived half an hour later to find message from Hugh saying that the manager of his hotel would be delighted to offer me a room for the night at a special reduced rate. Immediately made an excuse about a sick relative, checked out of Browning and set off for Hugh's hotel.

The reception staff made me most welcome and showed me up to a magnificent room with private bathroom on the first floor overlooking the Grand Canal. There was even a large bowl of flowers with the compliments of the management.

Shaved, dressed, picked one of the flowers for my buttonhole and rang Hugh's room. No reply. Surprised to find myself at the restaurant before him. Ordered a nice table for two, a Campari and soda, and waited. An hour later he still had not arrived, so I ordered. By 10.15 I had finished my meal and there was still no sign of him, so I paid my bill and returned to the hotel. Had been sitting in the lounge for half an hour when he walked in looking, I thought, rather tight.

'Where the hell did you get to?' he called out at the top of his voice.

I replied calmly that I had been at the Colomba, as arranged, and more to the point where the hell had *he* got to?

'The Colomba?' he exclaimed. 'I said quite clearly Al Colombo. Too bad. Carlo and his wife were there and invited me to join them. He was absolutely fascinating about Tintoretto and Canaletto. Right up your street.'

I asked him if he had said anything about the horses.

'No,' he said.

# *May*

## Monday, May 1st

May Day. An annual reminder of how lucky I was to have been born in England, and not in Russia.

Woken early by waiter banging on my door by mistake with someone else's breakfast.

By nine-thirty still no news from Carlo about the horses, so decided to go sightseeing alone. Arrived at Accademia to find it was closed all day Monday. Returned to the hotel around noon meaning to give Bryant-Fenn a piece of my mind, but he had gone out.

Presented with my bill. Even with the 75 per cent reduction, it came to far more than the Browning. As it was, I finished up with only 200 lire in my pocket, which meant that until Hugh paid me back, I would not be able to buy presents for Jane, etc.

Hugh finally appeared carrying a lot of parcels. 'Oh, there you are,' he said. 'I've just been to San Giorgio. The Carpaccios were looking better than ever. You really missed something.'

I said that, thanks to him, there was scarcely a thing in Venice that I had *not* missed.

'Oh, I wouldn't say that, old man,' he replied cheerfully. 'If it hadn't been for me, you'd never have had such a cheap night in this hotel, and you certainly never would have got to Torcello.' I pointed out that that might well be so, but at least I'd have had some money left over to do some shopping.

Hugh said, 'If you'd called up this morning before rushing out, I could have paid you back. I changed a couple of travellers' cheques last night. As it was, I assumed you were all right, so I blew the lot on a set of Murano wine glasses. Never mind, I'll write you a cheque in London. Wouldn't want you to be out of pocket.'

I am not a man who bears a grudge, but I simply could not bring myself to speak to him or even look him in the face all the way out to the airport.

In the lounge he offered to buy me a farewell drink. 'Never let it be said that I cannot stand my turn,' he said. Even so, he was short and I had to give him my last 200 lire to make up the difference. Our flight was being called when I felt a tap on my shoulder. Turned to find Carlo and his wife. 'Sorry you couldn't make the horses,' he said. 'They were fascinating.'

I was astounded and said I thought it was all off.

Carlo said, 'But didn't you get my message at the hotel? Hugh assured me last night you would receive it first thing this morning.'

I turned to Hugh for an explanation, but all he said was, 'I've been meaning to remove my custom from that hotel for years. The rooms and the food are marvellous, but the service is terrible.' How fortunate I am not to have to depend on freeloading for my livelihood. It leads only to dissatisfaction and meanness. I shall certainly not travel under similar conditions again.

## Tuesday, May 2nd

An astonishing piece of news. Beddoes is to join the European Commission at a salary of £20000 a year, tax free, if you please. He takes up his new post in Brussels in the middle of June. He announced this when he got in from the office this evening. Naturally I said that I was very pleased for him and offered him my warmest congratulations – although frankly I should have thought that the sum total of his knowledge of the Common Market, not to say foreign languages, could be jotted down on the back of a postage stamp.

A more pressing worry, however, is what will happen to the flat? Jane and I certainly could not afford to keep it up on our own, and I do not relish the prospect of sharing it with people we do not know. The first week of May should bring with it a prospect of blue skies and warm days; instead all I can see ahead are the black clouds and cold winds of uncertainty.

Is it my imagination, or did I read somewhere that there is a thriving market for blue movies in Belgium?

## Wednesday, May 3rd

Is it any wonder people are so depressed these days? Set off at lunchtime to buy a birthday present for my nephew who is seven on Saturday. With James Joyce for a name, what else could one give him but books?

In the bookshop near the office I was confronted by an eager young assistant with a moustache. I told him that I was looking for Arthur Ransome.

'Does he work here?' the young man enquired.

I told him no, Arthur Ransome, the author.

'What sort of things does he write, sir?' he asked.

At first I assumed he was trying to be funny. However, it soon became clear that, despite my mentioning some of the better-known titles and a brief résumé of the plot of *Pigeon Post*, he had never heard of either the author or the books. Finally, between us, we succeeded in locating a shelf full of Ransomes, and I chose *Winter Holiday* and *The Picts and the Martyrs*. As he was wrapping them, he confessed that today was his first day in the shop and that anyway he was there only on a temporary basis.

I asked him what he did normally and he told me he was studying at the Open University.

'What subject?' I asked him.

'English literature,' he replied.

I was sorely tempted to ask him if he had ever heard of William Wordsworth, but felt I had probably made my point sufficiently strongly already.

## Thursday, May 4th

To drinks at the Pedalows'. In view of Tim's gross mishandling of my portfolio, I had made up my mind not to go – a decision I knew I should have stuck to the moment I set foot through the front door. What Vanessa had described gaily as 'a few close friends' turned out to be half the stock exchange.

Tim thrust a glass of champagne in my hand with the instruction to 'go on up', and disappeared into the arms of a tall, rather common-looking blonde towing an even taller man in Gucci shoes and hair that curled under his ears.

Made my way up the stairs to the sitting room on the first floor, to be faced by a large room jammed to the door with shouting, smoking party-goers. The couple near the door stared at me coldly. I took one look, turned, and walked quickly downstairs to the dining room, which by now was as full as the sitting room. An arm in a white sleeve reached out with a champagne bottle and attempted to refill my glass. I waved it away impatiently and a voice said, 'You're getting very grand in your old age, aren't you?'

Turned to find the waiter grinning at me in a knowing sort of way. I was in no mood for badinage with the staff and frowned at him coldly.

'You don't recognize me, do you?' the waiter said.

I confessed that I did not.

'School House?' he said. 'Togger's Room? 1955?'

It still meant nothing to me, and I shook my head.

'You must remember,' he said. 'Maddocks, C. M.'

I said, 'Not Wanker Maddocks?'

His face positively lit up at this and he said, 'I knew it would all come back eventually.'

It didn't, as a matter of fact, since as far as I could recall he had been in a quite different set from me at school and I had barely exchanged two words with him the whole time we were there. Even so, it did not particularly surprise me that he should be a waiter at a party where I was a guest. I decided to cut the conversation short by telling him that if he stuck at it he'd probably do very well one day.

'Oh, I'm doing quite well already,' he replied. 'I very rarely take home less than three hundred a week.'

I was so taken aback I could hardly speak.

'Do you ever go back to the school?' he enquired.

I said that, as far as I was concerned, a man who kept returning to the scenes of his childhood was unlikely ever to get on in the world. Maddocks said, 'I wouldn't know about that. I cater for all the Old Boys' Dinners now, and I clear enough from them to pay for a month's holiday in Barbados every year.'

He then handed me a business card saying, 'You might be very glad of this one of these days,' and made off into the crowd brandishing his champagne bottle. Now I come to think about it, he was reputed in Togger's to have been half Jewish, if not wholly so.

## Friday, May 5th

My birthday. I can hardly believe I am thirty-six. I do not feel a day over twenty.

Cards from mother, Nigel and Priscilla, Mollie Marsh-Gibbon, and Mrs Veal.

Jane, looking quite attractive for once, gave me a scarf which she had knitted herself. I was quite touched and asked her to have dinner with me. She accepted immediately.

Beddoes strolled in smoking a cigar and threw a small parcel into my lap saying, 'Many happy returns, matey.'

It was a pack of playing cards with a couple on the reverse side involved in a series of sexual acts. If you arrange the cards in a certain order and then flick them, the couple perform as though in a film.

The man involved was unrecognizable, but just for fun I asked Beddoes if this was by way of being a personal show reel. However, he did not rise to the bait so I let the matter drop.

As he was leaving he said, 'Oh, by the way, this is also for you. It came while you were away.' And he tossed another small parcel on to the table.

I opened it up to find inside a pair of plastic bloomers plus a leaflet which explained that if you inflate them and then do a number of prescribed exercises in them, 'You will see the inches literally melting away from your waist and hips.'

I detect the hand of Armitage in this.

Had planned to confront him with them, but then he and the others in the office invited me out for a celebratory lunchtime drink at the Stoat and Anvil, so had to postpone it. As it turned out, he spoiled the whole occasion by getting tight and trying to persuade all the other customers to join in singing 'Happy Birthday to You'. But then, of course, if you're the chairman's nephew you can get away with anything.

To dinner with Jane at the San Sebastiano off Beauchamp Place. Aside from bumping into Armitage, a most promising start to my thirty-seventh year, and to the renaissance of our romance.

## Saturday, May 6th

After breakfast, locked my bedroom door and tried on the plastic pants. Blew them up with special hand pump and had just embarked on first exercise when Jane called out that Tim was on the phone. I threw my dressing gown on and hurried into the sitting room. Jane there drinking coffee and reading the *Express*.

Tim unusually agitated. It appears that on a recent business trip to Germany, he started up a passionate affair with a blonde typist from Hamburg. He is keen to continue the relationship by letter and has suggested to her that she write to him c/o my flat. I was so astonished that I fell back into the nearest armchair.

Stupidly, I had clean forgotten the inflated plastic pants which exploded with a loud report, causing Jane to tip coffee all over herself and Beddoes to come rushing in, stark naked, thinking someone had been shot. I could hear Tim's voice calling out, 'What's happening, what's happening?'

I shouted back, 'I've finally exploded,' and put down the phone.

I am still very much in two minds what to say to Tim. One thing I do know: there is no danger of my ever becoming a sexual deviant – at least in plastic.

## Sunday, May 7th

On a whim, decided to drive down to my old school. Terrible traffic in south London, and arrived only just in time for Maters. Was parking in Pegram's Piece when I realized with a shock that this was the first time I had been back in seventeen years. It felt most peculiar walking into chapel in a double-breasted suit without having to worry about how many buttons I had done up. Service most disappointing. Singing very thin and ragged compared with my day. Tried to set an example by shouting out the descants in 'Guide Me, O Thou Great Redeemer', as we always used to do, only to discover that I was absolutely on my own. The whole school turned round and stared at me. I have never felt such a fool in my life. Sermon by Head Magister similarly second-rate.

Afterwards bumped into Dickie Dunmow, of all people, in Apthorpe's Bottom. Went straight up and introduced myself. At first he had difficulty placing me, but then he remembered me absolutely and said that I might be interested to know that my record for the lowest mark ever achieved in A-level Latin verse still stood. He asked me what I was up to now and when I told him, he said gloomily, 'No more than I would have predicted, and no less.'

I should have known it's always a great mistake to go back, and I decided the time had come to return to London. For old times' sake, exercised my privilege of strolling across the grass in Upper Bummers with my hands in my pockets, as I had done countless times on my way to Sunday Refec. Was halfway across, reflecting dreamily on the old days, when I heard a voice calling out, 'Excuse me, but visitors are not allowed on the grass.'

Turned to see a Top Swine striding towards me, his blue gown flapping behind him. I pointed out that as an OF who had in his time been a Top Swine, a Swotbag *and* in the Upper Sixth, the term 'visitor' was hardly applicable. The boy said, in an insolent tone of voice, 'Well, you're not any of those things now, are you?'

For two pins I'd have boxed his ears, but I kept my temper and pointed out that he obviously knew nothing of Common Law under which a privilege, once granted, can never be removed. The boy replied that, as a matter of fact, he had been taking Law as an optional second subject instead of Estate Agency for the last two years, and he had never come across anything like that in his textbooks. He then suggested that I might perhaps like to discuss the matter further with the Head Magister.

I had better things to do than waste my time on such infantile argy-bargy, and, giving him a cold stare, I walked away towards my car in dignified silence. Nevertheless, I have no intention of letting the school get away with it scot free, and this evening I wrote a stiff letter to the Secretary of the OF Society cancelling my membership, my free copy of the School mag, and my standing order for the New Bilge Lab Fund. I also tore up Wanker Maddocks's visiting card into small pieces and threw them into the waste-paper basket.

## Monday, May 8th

Thirty-three years ago the German High Command surrendered to Field Marshal Montgomery at Lüneberg Heath. It seems scarcely credible. I never actually met Monty personally, although I did once see him at Windsor at the Garter ceremony for which Auntie Bettie had managed to get us tickets. Although not physically large, he gave the impression of being a big man in every sense of the word. He was often accused of being a cold, rather remote figure. I must say, that was not my experience at all; rather the contrary. I remember that when I called out, 'Good old Monty,' he broke off a conversation he was having with Winston and looked straight at me. And although I would not go so far as to say that he actually smiled, there was no doubt whatever about the keen personal interest he took in people from quite different walks of life from his own. I miss him.

## Tuesday, May 9th

Whether it was the memories of the great Allied victory that preoccupied my thoughts yesterday or what, I do not know, but the fact is that I have had the strangest feeling all today that something important and momentous is about to happen to me. And yet it has turned out to be one of the dullest and most uneventful days I can remember for a very long time.

## Wednesday, May 10th

The morning post brings a letter addressed to Tim Pedalow and bearing a German stamp. I have been giving this matter a certain amount of serious thought in the last few days, and while I am far from happy at the idea of acting as a private *poste restante* for the furtherance of Tim's extra-marital sexual liaisons, I have known him for very much longer than I have known Vanessa, and therefore I suppose that my loyalties should be more towards him than towards her. Besides, I daresay it's all fairly harmless.

Rang Tim who rushed in on his way home from the office, tore open the letter and sat on the edge of my bed wearing as silly an expression as I have seen on a grown man in a long time. He read it through no less than three times, then said he thought it would be better if I were to keep all the letters here for the time being. I told him he was a swine, to which he replied, 'I know. Don't you wish you were one, too?'

I replied that I wished for nothing less and that, in my view, if one really loved a woman, one did not gad about with bits on the side. Tim said, 'That's the trouble with all bachelors. They're hopeless idealists. Show me a man who has stayed faithful to his wife through the years, and I will show you a man who is sexually impotent.'

I was speechless.

As he was leaving, he said, 'Don't worry. I'll make it worth your while.'

I was sorely tempted to remind him that the last time he said that, he lost me £420, but really what is the point in trying to reason with those sort of people? Even so, his remarks have set me thinking again about the advisability of tying myself up permanently with Jane. But as things stand, what is the alternative?

## Thursday, May 11th

When I take stock in years to come, today will, without any question, stand out as the happiest and most momentous of my life. I still cannot quite believe my good fortune. Arrived at the Varney-Birches' dinner party rather late to find everyone already at table and halfway through the artichoke soup. Took my seat, rather hot and flustered, turned to the girl on my left to apologize, and found myself face to face with the love of my life.

Her name is Amanda Trubshawe, and she is not only very beautiful, but she happens to be the daughter, no less, of my chairman, and Armitage's uncle, Derek Trubshawe. The coincidence is too extraordinary for words. Even more extraordinary is the very idea that this exquisite creature of eighteen with her round, childlike face, enormous green eyes, and her long slim legs should be even remotely related to Armitage – let alone his first cousin.

I could not take my eyes off her all evening, nor she off me, and as far as I can remember, neither of us exchanged a single word with anyone else.

As I was waiting in the hall afterwards for Amanda to collect her coat prior to driving her home, Nan Varney-Birch came up and said, 'Normally I charge ten per cent for this kind of service, but you two looked so sweet, I'll only charge you five.'

I laughed, but secretly thought her rather common.

Obviously it was quite out of the question to take Amanda back to the flat for coffee. However, she seemed perfectly content to be driven straight home. I said that I imagined she had to be up early in the morning for work. She replied, 'Oh, I don't work. I'm doing the Season.'

I said, 'How extraordinary, so am I. Let's do it together.'

And she laughed and said, 'Yes, let's.'

The Trubshawes live in an enormous house in The Boltons. Amanda said she would have asked me in for a drink, only her father always sets the burglar alarms at eleven. I laughed and said I didn't mind at all, and we kissed.

As she was getting out of the car, she said, 'I hope you don't mind my mentioning it, but either your suit needs cleaning, or else there's a very peculiar smell in this car.'

I apologized and assured her I would be changing the car any day now – for a company car, a more ambitious man might have thought to himself as he drove away. But then very few men are lucky enough to be as much in love as I am.

## Friday, May 12th

Lay awake most of last night thinking alternately about Amanda, and poor old Jane. There's no doubt she has been making quite a play for me recently, and I could not bear to hurt her feelings. Slept fitfully and woke exhausted just before seven. Determined to tell Jane at the earliest opportunity. However, when she appeared at breakfast, she had so obviously made a special effort with her clothes and make-up, that I hadn't the heart to say anything. Another letter arrived for Tim from Germany. What a sordid business it all seems suddenly.

If only he had had the good fortune to marry a girl like Amanda, he would never have been forced to resort to this kind of cheap subterfuge. I feel sorry for him. Almost said something to Armitage about having met his cousin last night, but checked myself at the last moment.

Knowing him, he would almost certainly have found a way of using the information as a rod to beat my back. Stayed in all evening half hoping Amanda might ring, but no such luck. I would have rung her myself, but do not wish to appear too keen. To bed early with the *Evening Standard* and an apple.

## Saturday May 13th

Blew my nose so hard this morning I made it bleed. Rinsed the handkerchief immediately in cold water, but the stain had still not entirely disappeared, so popped it into a saucepan with some bleach to soak. Phone rang soon afterwards. It was Amanda inviting me to dine there this evening with her parents. My heart was beating so hard with the excitement that I felt sure she must have heard it on the other end of the line. Needless to say, accepted at once, and hurried out to buy Mrs Trubshawe some flowers.

Skipped along the street like a mad thing, singing and waving at everyone who passed. So anxious to share my happiness with others that, as I was overtaking one man, I gave him a cheery slap on the back. What I did not realize until too late was that he was carrying an enormous parcel of shopping, which he promptly dropped, spilling groceries and vegetables all over the pavement. I was sorry he chose to take it quite so badly.

Arrived back in the flat rather later than expected with a huge bunch of mixed roses. Went to deal with my hand-kerchief only to discover that it had dissolved into a mass of holes, at the same time making a funny mark on the bottom of the saucepan. Cleaned it out as best I could and made a mental note not to use that one for cooking. Noticed later that Beddoes used it for scrambled eggs, but said nothing. Car decided to pick this evening, of all evenings, to let me down, so forced to resort to a taxi.

Arrived at The Boltons to discover I had come out without any money. Nasty scene with the taxi driver who got very hot under the collar and called me all the names under the sun.

'You're all the same, you lot,' he shouted, gesturing

towards the Trubshawes' front door. 'Honesty's just a word to you.'

I pretended to be a total stranger to the neighbourhood and eventually he drove off grumbling and swearing. Try as I might, I simply cannot find it in my heart to like the working classes. Amanda met me at the door looking enchanting in blue, and took me through to the sitting room where she introduced me to her parents.

The chairman, a large, craggy man, said, 'We haven't met,' which was true. Indeed he seemed scarcely aware of my existence within the organization. When I reminded him I was in Armitage's group he said, 'I'm sorry to hear that.'

I said that I had understood that his nephew was doing very well.

'If you believe that,' he grunted, 'you'll believe anything.'

So astonished was I that I almost forgot to say good evening to Mrs Trubshawe who was seated in a large, squashy armchair by the fireplace. She was much younger than I had expected and in many ways just as attractive as her daughter.

I happened to notice she was wearing a rather unusual pair of lace-up boots and said I had never seen anything quite like them before.

Amanda said, 'They're a form of surgical boot. Mummy has to wear them for support. She broke her leg very badly last Christmas running for a taxi outside Peter Jones.'

I apologized for my tactlessness and said I was quite sure she had recovered by now.

'I haven't, as a matter of fact,' she said. 'Hence these hideous boots.'

Dinner was a simple affair: smoked salmon, tournedos Rossini, raspberries and cream, with Krug '66 and Château Mouton Rothschild, served by two oriental women in black frocks and white aprons. The Trubshawes asked me a number of personal questions, relating to my family and education.

On hearing that I was up at Oxford in the mid-sixties, they enquired if I had known someone called Arthur Croucher. I replied that I had not, but that with a splendidly Dickensian sounding name like that, he should go far. Enid Trubshawe said that was hardly likely since he was the only son of their dearest friends and had been killed in a car accident in Spain ten years ago.

Fortunately, things began to look up slightly when I mentioned my interest in the theatre. The chairman said, 'My wife likes to go. I normally get enough theatre during the day to last me for weeks.'

Enid asked me what playwrights I particularly admired. I thought for a while and finally said, 'Alan Bennett.'

The chairman grunted and said, 'Bennett, eh?'

It was difficult to tell from his tone of voice whether my answer had been very good or very bad.

Afterwards Amanda and her mother disappeared to make the coffee and the chairman took me into his study where he asked me a number of searching questions about the work of my group and the Barford project in particular. He then offered me a glass of his best brandy.

As I was leaving, Amanda said, 'They really like you.'

I said, 'Are you sure?'

She said, 'Yes, but not half as much as I do.'

I danced all the way home, swinging on the lamp-posts.

## Sunday, May 14th

Hugh Bryant-Fenn called round this morning to say he had a couple of free press passes to the Chelsea Flower Show tomorrow, if I was interested. I certainly am.

Every year I see those tents going up in Royal Hospital Gardens, and every year I promise myself I will go, but somehow I never seem to get round to it.

As Hugh himself pointed out, not only are the flowers at their freshest on the Monday, but it is traditionally the day on which the Queen pays a visit – presumably to plan her famous herbaceous border at the Palace.

Not that I would expect to meet her personally, but you can never tell with the Royal Family. They are becoming more relaxed and informal by the day. At all events, it is not everyone who is afforded the opportunity to launch into the London Season in such an auspicious manner.

Told Beddoes who said, 'What do you want to waste your time there for? You don't even have a window box.'

I tapped the side of my nose and said, 'I may have considerably more than a window box before long.'

Naturally he wanted to know what I meant by that, but I said, 'Never you mind,' and left him to stew in his own juice.

I cannot help feeling that he is unlikely to get far in Brussels if he does not take drastic steps to curb his tongue. I understand that tact and decorum are very much the key words in the social life of the Commission.

Rang Amanda to invite her to Chelsea with me tomorrow, but unfortunately she had promised to go with her parents on Tuesday which is the Society Day, whatever that may mean.

Wrote a long and, I think, rather witty thank-you letter to the Trubshawes. Must remember to post it tomorrow.

## Monday, May 15th

To Chelsea by taxi at four. I do not think I have been inside a tent of such proportions since I last went to Bertram Mills's Circus as a small boy.

The arrangement around the memorial column in the centre was particularly impressive. None of the exhibitors' names meant anything to me. Not that it mattered. I simply wandered about as the mood took me, smelling a rose here, admiring a rockery there, as I would in somebody's private garden.

Surprised to find workmen still busy constructing some of the stands. Also many fewer people than I had expected for the opening day. Commented on this to one of the rose growers who told me that it was only press day, and that it is tomorrow that all the nobs come.

I said that if Her Majesty wasn't a nob, I'd like to know who was, and enquired casually if she'd been yet. 'She always comes at five-thirty sharp,' he told me. 'That's why everyone's rushing to get their stands finished.' Could not help congratulating myself on having timed my own visit to coincide with the Royal Party's, and set off to look at some greenhouses.

Bumped into Philippe de Grande-Hauteville who said, 'I suppose you must be covering this for the Beeb.' Bloody fool.

Was on my way back into the tent when an official stepped forward and asked me to leave. I pointed out that I was not just any old passer-by off the street but an official member of the press, and I showed him my invitation. 'I don't care if you're Lord Beaverbrook,' he said. 'The rule is that everyone has to be out of here before the Queen arrives, and that means everyone, sunshine.'

I said that I could perfectly well understand Her Majesty wishing her visit to be of a private nature, but that I could not help thinking how distressed she would be to hear that members of the public, not to say the press, were treated with such discourtesy on her behalf. 'If that's all she has to worry about this week,' the official said, 'she can count herself lucky.'

I somehow managed to control my temper, but unfortunately in doing so gave myself another nasty nosebleed.

Walked up to Peter Jones to buy some handkerchiefs and browse round Smith's for half an hour before catching the 19 bus down the King's Road.

Immediately became stuck in the most appalling traffic jam. When I complained to the conductor, he said, 'What can you expect when the Queen goes to Chelsea in the middle of the rush hour?'

I'm not blaming Her Majesty, but it is incidents like this that cause one to wonder if the monarchy is not more trouble than it is worth.

The moment I got home, I jotted down a verbatim account of both incidents and penned a stiff letter on the subject to *The Times*. I have a feeling it could stir up quite a controversy.

Nose still bleeding slightly.

## Tuesday, May 16th

Mollie Marsh-Gibbon rang to say she had a spare guest ticket for Chelsea, if I was interested. I described my previous day's experience and said I was not surprised the London Season had declined if that was the sort of treatment one could expect.

'My dear fellow,' she shrieked, 'for one thing Chelsea has never been considered part of the Season; the Academy Exhibition is traditionally the opening event. And secondly, what can you expect if you will go on Press Day? Half the stands are still being built, the place is swarming with half-naked workmen and seedy photographers, and the flowers are only half out. The point is, the whole thing is geared to today when all the members of the RHS go, not to the Queen.'

I daresay Mollie is right. She usually is, which is maddening. Even so, I sometimes wonder if she has a good word to say for anyone.

Have not blown nose all day, and nose-bleed quite cleared up.

## Wednesday, May 17th

Quite without thinking, gave nose hard blow on waking up, with disastrous results. Two more letters have arrived from Germany – a bitter reminder that I still have not broken the news to Jane about Amanda. Oddly enough, she has never looked more cheerful, and when I said how sorry I was not to have seen much of her lately, she seemed remarkably unconcerned. No sign of my letter yet in *The Times*.

## Thursday, May 18th

Unable to find a clean handkerchief anywhere, so had to set off to work without one – a thing I have not done for many years. I felt as uncomfortable as if I had gone to the office without any underpants. Not that I have ever gone to the office without my underpants, or anywhere else for that matter – although I understand there are people who do.

## Friday, May 19th

By a curious coincidence, my rash has suddenly taken it into its head to return. Whether this is due, in some psychological way, to my thinking about not wearing underpants yesterday, or simply because of the unusually warm weather, I do not know. At all events, it is extremely irritating, in every sense of the word.

So, too, is the non-appearance of my letter in *The Times*.

## Saturday, May 20th

Have been feeling rather faint and dizzy all day – probably as a result of losing so much blood. It has hardly been the most propitious start to the Season. However, I would rather be physically below par than mentally – which is what Tim obviously is. He arrived this morning to collect the latest outpourings from his Teutonic paramour, and announced that he had decided to take all the letters home with him. I asked him if this was really wise to which he replied, 'If we all confined ourselves only to what is wise, nothing would ever get done in this world.'

I said that considering I had risked, and very nearly lost, £500 at his hands, that remark was singularly ill-advised. He replied, 'Pah. What's five hundred these days?'

I told him a great deal to some people, and that he need not expect me to risk my good name, or my savings, on his behalf again in a hurry. He left without another word.

After tea, while soaking handkerchiefs, wrote a stiff note to the editor of *The Times*, reminding him of the public's enormous interest in all matters relating to the Royal Family, and drawing his attention to my letter of the 15th.

## Sunday, May 21st

Vanessa rang after breakfast to say that she had just found Tim's letters in a box under the bed, and that not only was she leaving Tim, but she never wanted to speak to me again as long as she lived.

I attempted to defend myself but found I was speaking into a dead telephone.

Was so angry and upset I simply could not bring myself to have a heart to heart with Jane this evening, as I had planned. As it happened, she went out anyway. She always seems to be going out these days.

On the subject of letters, I am reminded that I never actually heard that I had *not* won the Wildlife Game. What a joy to have some clean handkerchiefs at last.

## Monday, May 22nd

To the Royal Academy with Amanda for the opening day of the Summer Exhibition. The Season is well and truly under way at last, and despite everything that has happened in the last few days, I could not be more cheerful.

It's extraordinary to think that in all the years I have lived

'. . . to my astonishment found myself face to face with a portrait of Dickie Dunmow, of all people.'

in London, I have never actually set foot inside the Academy. Every year I plan to go to the Summer Exhibition, and every year they take it off before I have had the chance to get round to it. I daresay it's a problem many busy people experience. Still, better not to go at all than rush off willy-nilly to absolutely everything that comes on, like some people I know.

Entrance hall swarming with people. Surprised and disappointed not to recognize any famous society faces in the crowd. Also surprised that the so-called security men did not give us a second glance as we entered the building. Just because neither of us was carrying a brief case or a carrier bag did not mean that we could not have been concealing a bread knife or a razor blade somewhere about our persons. After what happened to Rembrandt's 'Night Watch' in the Rijks-museum in Amsterdam, you'd have thought they'd have learned their lesson.

Paused briefly at the top of the stairs where they were selling catalogues, but did not bother to buy one myself. If a painting is not immediately self-explanatory, it is probably not worth bothering about anyway.

Amanda, I am glad to say, is of the same opinion. Entered the first room and to my astonishment found myself face to face with a portrait of Dickie Dunmow, of all people. The artist's name meant nothing to me, but I must congratulate him on achieving an excellent likeness, especially from a distance.

I was only sorry to see that it was not for sale, otherwise I might have been tempted to purchase it myself. Realizing that the man standing beside me was also admiring the portrait, I said to him, 'It may interest you to know that that man was my Latin beak at school.'

He stared at me for a moment, said something in a foreign language, and walked away. I simply do not understand why foreigners bother to come to traditional English events like the Summer Exhibition if they have not the slightest interest in learning about the English way of life.

At one point listened to two middle-aged women in hats discussing a picture and distinctly heard one of them say, 'In a way it's rather like going to see *Electra*. If you're not up in Sophocles, you probably won't understand the half of it.' The painting under debate was a self-portrait of a naked man standing in front of a bedroom mirror. Two women could be seen out of the window, gardening. The only thing I could not understand was why, on a nice sunny day, the painter was not out there in the fresh air with them instead of fiddling about indoors.

Very disappointed by the depressingly low standard of dress of most of the people present. Few of the men were wearing ties and many of the women actually had on T-shirts and jeans. I felt positively over-dressed in my pin-stripe suit.

We can only hope for better things at Ascot.

## Tuesday, May 23rd

Was describing my experiences at the Academy to Sarah over coffee this morning when Armitage marched in and said that if it was big hats and social chit-chat I was after, I should have gone to the Private View Day, which was last Thursday. Since I have been quite unable to take anything Armitage says seriously after the recent conversation with his uncle, I merely ignored him and left the room.

Enid Trubshawe rang in the afternoon to thank me for the unexpected letter describing my experiences at the Chelsea Flower Show, and to ask me to the theatre tomorrow night. I was so dumb-struck on both counts that I completely forgot to ask what the play was. Wondered about dropping a line to the editor of *The Times* explaining that there had been a mix-up in the letters, but finally decided we both have enough on our plates as it is.

## Wednesday, May 24th

Arrived at The Boltons in good time for a drink, as instructed. No sign of Amanda or the chairman. When I remarked on this, Enid said coolly, 'It's just the two of us. I hope you're not one of these people who has old-fashioned scruples about going out alone with married women.'

I replied that I had for some reason expected a small party. She laughed lightly and said, 'How sweet. I do believe you're blushing.'

Frankly I was beginning to feel rather uncomfortable at the somewhat suggestive tone of the conversation, and pointed out that if we wanted to be at the Lyric in time for the curtain, we had better go.

I remember very little of the play or of our supper afterwards at the Ivy, except that I had the impression Enid touched me on the arm rather more often than was necessary, and on one or two occasions deliberately pressed her leg against mine under the table. We arrived back at The Boltons at midnight to find the chairman still not back from his business dinner and Amanda still out at her girls' bridge party. Naturally, I did not wish to be caught in a compromising situation; on the other hand, it is never advisable to give a frustrated middle-aged woman the cold shoulder. In the end settled for a neat compromise by announcing that I had to be up early for a meeting and kissing her on the hand.

She said, 'I think that, under the circumstances, a chaste kiss on the cheek might be more in order.'

I had no alternative but to oblige.

On my way home in the taxi, I found myself thinking more and more about the phrase 'under the circumstances'. What precisely did she mean by this? Was she referring to my friendship with Amanda and looking forward to the time when she would be my mother-in-law? Was she perhaps in the habit of being taken to the theatre by young men and being kissed afterwards on the sofa? Or was she simply implying that some sort of relationship between us had been set in motion? And, if so, where does that leave me *vis-à-vis* Amanda? Am I expected to carry on with the two of them at the same time, or are the Trubshawes one of these sexy families one reads about for whom anything goes?

My head is in a complete whirl, and matters are not helped by the realization that in fact I am as attracted to Enid as I am to her daughter, if not more so.

How difficult these affairs of the heart can be. One sometimes wonders if they are not more trouble than they're worth.

## Thursday, May 25th

Hugh Bryant-Fenn rang almost as soon as I got in this morning and said in a facetious tone of voice, 'Who was that lady I saw you with last night?'

I replied that I hadn't the faintest idea what he was talking about. 'Don't be silly,' he said. 'That gorgeous older number you were being so intimate with in the dress circle of the Lyric.'

His suggestive manner, combined with the fact that he had still made no effort to repay me the money I lent him in Venice, made my hackles rise, and I told him sharply that if it was any business of his she was my aunt up from Leighton Buzzard for the day.

Hugh laughed and said, 'Aunt, my big toe. Aunts don't look at nephews like that.'

I replied that I was not in the habit of discussing my private affairs with people who owed me money, and put the phone down on him.

Armitage looked in a couple of times, but I pretended I was too busy to speak to him. He seemed to me to have a peculiarly crafty look on his face that I have not noticed before. Does he know something?

Not a word all day from Amanda. Does she know something? The only person who certainly knows nothing is the unfortunate Jane.

This evening Beddoes made a coarse joke about a Negro and a ship's captain which I did not get. He tells me he is to start taking evening classes in French on Monday, which I suppose is something to be thankful for.


## Friday, May 26th

Now the cat is really out of the bag. Was working on the revised Barford figures this morning when Armitage walked in, threw a newspaper down on my desk with the words, 'You're for the high jump now,' and marched out again.

The paper was open at the gossip column. Ran my eyes quickly over the various items but could find nothing that concerned me. Finally, my eye was caught by a brief paragraph at the bottom of the page, which read:

Is the rather continental fashion of young men squiring older women around town beginning to make a comeback after all these years? Eligible marketing executive, Simon Cusp, 36, who was seen in intimate conversation with Mrs Enid Trubshawe last night at the Ivy, once London's most fashionable after-theatre supper place, had a strangely pre-war look about him. Mrs Trubshawe, 46, wife of Harley Preston chairman, and sometime Conservative candidate, Derek Trubshawe, was formerly musical comedy actress Enid Trehearne, which perhaps accounts for her old-fashioned theatrical tastes.

I had often wondered what it feels like to achieve sudden overnight fame, but had never dreamed of it happening in quite this way. Needless to say, I was shocked and horrified at the appalling implications.

Obviously my career is in ruins.

My romance with Amanda is at an end, as are any chances I might have from now on of making a good marriage. My friends will never let me hear the end of it, and it may be many months before I can go down to Kent again.

On the other hand, I must admit that I am rather excited at being mentioned in such a famous gossip column and am only sorry that they spelt my name wrong.

Decided to adopt the tactics traditionally employed by those involved in scandals, and disappeared – firstly into a pub unfrequented by people from the office and thence into the dark anonymity of the Academy Cinema. Unfortunately realized too late that they were showing *Les Enfants du Paradis* which I have seen three times and have never much cared for anyway.

Stayed in all evening, but although the phone rang several times, not once was it for me. I daresay the Trubshawe family is suffering enough agony as it is without my adding to it. Quite unable to concentrate on any TV programme, so tidied my room instead. Found myself looking at my possessions as if for the last time.

## Saturday, May 27th

Have always believed that the best form of defence is attack, so after breakfast took my courage in both hands and rang the Trubshawes. Enid answered. She sounded strained and tired – quite unlike her usual bubbling self. I said, 'I have been thinking things over and have decided to go abroad for a while.'

There was a long pause from the other end and then the voice said, 'I see. Well, they're all away for the weekend, too.

On the Hamble. I'll tell them when they get back tomorrow, shall I?'

I told whoever it was that it didn't matter and rang off. Spent the rest of the day in an agony of doubt and self-reproach. Jane seemed at a loose end, too, for once and under the circumstances decided I had nothing to lose by asking her out to dinner and did so.

I was surprised that, having made such an effort with her appearance over the last week or so, she seemed to have made almost none this evening. But then it was not as though we were going to the Savoy – or the Ivy.

## Sunday, May 28th

Woke this morning with a terrible pain in my chest. Thought at first I might have suffered a mild heart attack but decided it was probably only indigestion.

I have finally come to the conclusion that I do not like Indian food.

Read the papers in a desultory way and walked in Holland Park with Jane. Saw a dog that reminded me very much of the Trubshawes' West Highland. Bent down to stroke its head and it bit me on the hand quite sharply.

As if mental pain were not enough.

## Monday, May 29th

The call came at last at half-past ten. As I was going up to the fourteenth floor in the lift, I reflected how ironical it was that the only time I should set foot in the chairman's office was in order to be asked to leave.

And to think that less than a week ago he was well on his way to becoming my father-in-law.

Under the circumstances he seemed remarkably cheerful. Before I could utter a word, he said, 'I've been thinking things over at the weekend and have come to the conclusion that the best answer would be to shovel Colin off into Merchandising Development and move you up to Assistant Group Head. That way, no one's going to get shirty.'

I was struck literally dumb for a moment or two and

stared at him in amazement. He asked me if I had any objections. Obviously he knew nothing of my relationship with his wife or of the newspaper item. I decided that there was no point in trying to pull the wool over his eyes any further. I said, 'I think I should tell you, sir, that your wife and I have struck up a relationship.'

'I should hope so, too. My wife is a very warm and open woman.'

I said, 'I am sure she is, sir, but I do not think you quite understand. On Wednesday night she and I went to the theatre alone and dined afterwards at the Ivy.'

'Excellent,' he exclaimed. 'I hope you had a good time. As I told you, I do not care for the theatre myself, and I am delighted that you enjoy it as much as she does. If you do become a member of the family one of these days, as seems likely, I'm sure there will be many opportunities for all three of you to go together.'

I could hardly believe my ears. Promotion and a virtual offer of marriage in one day. It was almost too much to take in at one go.

Even so, I felt it my duty to explain about the newspaper item, but all he said was, 'My wife still enjoys a little publicity from time to time. It wouldn't surprise me to learn that she'd rung up the paper herself.'

As I stood up to leave, my feet seemed scarcely to be touching the carpet, so intoxicating was my sense of relief and happiness. And as if that were not enough, he then asked me to join them all in their villa near Antibes on Saturday for a couple of weeks. Arrived back in the office to find Armitage emptying his desk. He seemed quite defeated and for once I actually felt quite sorry for him.

## Tuesday, May 30th

Unable to keep the news to myself any longer and told Beddoes quietly this evening of my good fortune. All he said was, 'Good. Perhaps now you can get on and find yourself a few decent mistresses.' I simply cannot imagine how I can have lived with him for all these years, and can only thank heaven that I shall not be doing so any longer.

## *Wednesday, May 31st*

Found myself alone in the flat with Jane for the first time in days and so was able finally to break the news to her. She said, 'I'm so glad. I hope you'll be as happy with her as I am with Colin Armitage.'

For the first time in my life, I was completely stuck for words.

# *June*

## *Thursday, June 1st*

Unable to get any serious work done all morning for reflecting on my future and the strange way life has of taking one completely unawares. One moment everything looks as black as it could be, and the next thing you know, the clouds have dispersed and all is sweetness and light. Less than a week ago, I seemed to be a man without any prospects, and now suddenly I am poised to make my mark on the world in no uncertain terms.

The way ahead is clear at last.

## *Friday, June 2nd*

The twenty-fifth anniversary of the Queen's Coronation, and a red letter day for me, too, since today I officially take up my position as Assistant Group Head with special responsibility for the Barford project. I have also decided to discontinue my diary. Obviously, from now on I shall have neither the time nor the need for introspection, and my mind will doubtless be occupied with more important matters than the trivial activities of my friends and acquaintances.

Amanda rang after lunch from Antibes to say that she and her father had decided at her mother's suggestion to fly on ahead, and did I mind terribly driving down slowly with Enid in the Rolls. I suppose this is wise?

Sorry to discover in the bath tonight that my rash still hasn't quite gone.

*Other Arrow Books of interest:*

# THE HISTORY MAN

## Malcolm Bradbury

Howard Kirk is the trendiest of radical tutors at a fashionable campus university. Timid Vice-Chancellors pale before his threats of disruption; reactionary colleagues are crushed beneath the weight of his merciless Marxist logic; women are irresistibly drawn by his progressive promiscuity.

A self-appointed revolutionary hero, Howard Kirk always comes out on top. And Malcolm Bradbury dissects him in this savagely funny novel that has been universally acclaimed as one of the masterpieces of the decade.

'A gold medal to Malcolm Bradbury for the funniest and best-written novel I have seen for a very long time.' Auberon Waugh, *Evening Standard*

'Extremely witty . . . Bradbury writes brilliantly' *New York Times*

**90p**

# EATING PEOPLE IS WRONG

## Malcolm Bradbury

Professor Treece is one of the most respected figures at a small provincial university – kingpin in the world of poetry readings, tea parties and excursions to Stratford. But with the onset of middle age, he is plagued by a sense of failure.

No one threatens him more than Louis Bates, the earnest and unattractive new student who attacks Treece's teaching and lifestyle. Treece is determined not to be upset by a mere freshman but sparks fly when they both fall in love with Emma, a desirable post-graduate . . .

'Immensely enjoyable . . . genuinely witty and frequently hilarious' *New York Times*

'The funniest book I have read this year' *Daily Telegraph*

£1·25

# STEPPING WESTWARD

## Malcolm Bradbury

'A wealth of comic inventions . . . utterly hilarious' *The Listener*

James Walker is a trapped man; a dispirited novelist living a drab life in a grey northern city. He's only in his early thirties yet he feels, tired, flabby, out-of-touch and fed up.

Walker's liberation is at hand. He is appointed Fellow of Creative Writing at an American University: and, once installed, finds that his image is now that of Resident Angry Young Man. Two affairs and several social gaffes later, he is beginning to suspect that there is more to the uninhibited campus lifestyle of the 'sixties than meets the eye.

£1.25

# NO MORE DYING THEN

## Ruth Rendell

The mysterious death of little Stella Rivers was still fresh in the minds of everyone who lived in Kingsmarkham. No one wanted a repetition of that harrowing time. So when a five-year-old boy vanished the whole police force moved feverishly into action.

Chief Inspector Wexford thinks he knows all the obvious places to search . . . and whom to suspect. But there are no clues whatsoever – none, that is, until the anonymous letters start arriving . . .

85p

# MURDER BEING ONCE DONE

## Ruth Rendell

'DEATH ONLY IS REAL'
So read the grim epitaph on a family vault. Appropriate
enough, for it was here, amid the decay and desolation of
Kenbourne Vale Cemetery, that the girl's body was found.

Detective Chief Inspector Wexford was in London for a rest
but he soon found himself deeply involved in this baffling
case.

85p

# BESTSELLERS FROM ARROW

All these books are available from your bookshop or newsagent or you can order them direct. Just tick the titles you want and complete the form below.

| | | | |
|---|---|---|---|
| ☐ | BEAUTIFUL JUST! | Lillian Beckwith | 60p |
| ☐ | EVEREST THE HARD WAY | Chris Bonington | £1.25 |
| ☐ | THE HISTORY MAN | Malcolm Bradbury | 95p |
| ☐ | A RUMOR OF WAR | Philip Caputo | £1.25 |
| ☐ | RAVEN | Shana Carrol | £1.50 |
| ☐ | 2001: A SPACE ODYSSEY | Arthur C. Clarke | 95p |
| ☐ | SAM 7 | Richard Cox | £1.25 |
| ☐ | BILLION DOLLAR KILLING | Paul Erdman | 95p |
| ☐ | ZULU DAWN | Cy Endfield | 95p |
| ☐ | BLAKES 7 | Trevor Hoyle | 95p |
| ☐ | IN GALLANT COMPANY | Alexander Kent | 95p |
| ☐ | CITY OF THE DEAD | Herbert Lieberman | £1.25 |
| ☐ | THE VALHALLA EXCHANGE | Harry Patterson | 80p |
| ☐ | SAVAGE SURRENDER | Natasha Peters | £1.60 |
| ☐ | STRUMPET CITY | James Plunkett | £1.50 |
| ☐ | SURFACE WITH DARING | Douglas Reeman | 85p |
| ☐ | A DEMON IN MY VIEW | Ruth Rendell | 65p |
| ☐ | THE SAVIOUR | Mark & Marvin Werlin | £1.25 |

Postage  _____

Total  _____

---

ARROW BOOKS, BOOKSERVICE BY POST, PO BOX 29, DOUGLAS, ISLE OF MAN, BRITISH ISLES

Please enclose a cheque or postal order made out to Arrow Books Limited for the amount due including 8p per book for postage and packing for orders within the UK and 10p for overseas orders.

Please print clearly

NAME ...............................................................................

ADDRESS ........................................................................

..............................................................................................

Whilst every effort is made to keep prices down and to keep popular books in print. Arrow Books cannot guarantee that prices will be the same as those advertised here or that the books will be available.